THIS MESS

THE DEVIL'S OUTLAWS
BOOK 3

BETHANY DAWN

To my Acey boy:
Some may say you were only a dog, and they would be fucking wrong. You were my son, and goddamn, losing you fucking hurt. I miss you bubs, I hope you're waiting for me somewhere 'cause I won't be at peace until I find you again.

TRIGGER WARNINGS

This is a series about a 1%er motorcycle club, please expect them to act accordingly. This Mess depicts grief, shitty parents, what some might consider verbal abuse, toxic af men, extreme acts of violence, recreational drug use, and explicit sex scenes. Please be conscious of your triggers, your mental health matters.

Bethany

PLAYLIST

Hurts So Good - Astrid S
In My Veins - Andrew Belle & Erin Mccarley
Let You Go - Machine Gun Kelly
Water Fountain - Alec Benjamin
@ My Worst - Blackbear
Is There Somewhere - Halsey
Habits - Machine Gun Kelly
Swim - Chase Atlantic
I'm Sick of Trying - Vaboh
Girls Like U - Blackbear
Make up sex - Machine Gun Kelly, Blackbear
Roses - GASHI

Playlist available on Spotify @bethanydawnn17

PREFACE

This is going to hurt.

1

SAINT

THE WORST PART ABOUT YOUR LOVED ONES DYING, OTHER THAN them being fucking dead, of course, is that while your world has come to a screeching halt—the entire world slamming into your back and knocking the breath right out of you—is that everyone else's worlds are continuing as normal. They don't feel the gaping hole that used to be filled with one of the best people alive. Their world just continues to spin, around and around.

As if you didn't already feel alone enough.

They'll be there for the funeral, and the days leading up to it, but after that you're alone, and everyone else has forgotten. How the fuck could they forget? They don't have to live in grief and anger; the questions that keep you up at night and wake you before your alarm with tears running down your face. Why me? Why them? Why now? Why?

My hand hits one of the wood doors of the Chapel, stopping my face from slamming into it as I sway on my feet, hanging on loosely to the neck of a bottle of Grey Goose. I twist the knob and push the door open, staring into the dark room. Slowly walking into the room, I flick on the light as I go, kicking the door shut with my boot and making my way to the head of the table. The room smells like smoke and a mixture of all of the guys' colognes. The loud music and sounds of the party fade away behind the thick doors. My ass hits my old seat hard, the one to the left of the head of the table, and I set the short tumbler on the table in front of his chair.

"This shouldn't be happening. You should be here, brother." The clear liquid pours into the glass tumbler. My eyes burn with the tears I haven't let myself release. "Goddamn it, I fucking miss you so much already, Ro." I take a gulp from the bottle, setting it down and resting my elbows on the table next to it. "How the fuck am I supposed to do this without you? Run this club, sit in your fucking chair?" I take another drink, the burn in my throat subsiding the more I drink. "We didn't finish the K-Model." A loud cheer seeps in under the door and catches my attention. I turn my stare back to the empty chair next to me, taking another drink. "You're the one person I want to talk to right now, and I fucking can't." My head falls to my open hands resting on the table. "I know all of us are going through this, but you were there from the beginning. You brought me into the club. Guided me. You made me into the man I am today." I lean back in my chair and pull the President patch out of my pocket, staring at it as I promise, "I'm gonna find who did this, Ro." I let out a heavy sigh. "I'm so fucking angry. You didn't deserve this. You were too great to go out like that; gunned down in a fucking alley by yourself." A tear falls down my face and I angrily wipe it away with the back of my hand. "Where was I, Ronan? Where the fuck was I!? I wasn't there and you were alone! You died alone! I should have been there!" I yell. "Fuck!" I throw the lone tumbler at the wall and it shatters.

"Whoa, what did that glass ever do to you?" A husky voice jokes, and I recognize it instantly; I could pick her out anywhere.

"What are you doing here, Allie?" I keep my gaze trained on

the wall, hoping she'll leave me alone to wallow in my anger and grief.

The door thunks closed and the soft click of her heels on the hardwood gets closer. Guess she's not leaving. "Avoiding flying glassware, apparently." I scoff but then her voice turns serious. "When I heard there was a party for your promotion I wanted to congratulate you, but this doesn't look like a happy occasion."

Scooting down in the chair, I rest my head on the back and close my eyes. "What gave it away?"

From the bottom of my eyesight, I can see Allie lean against the table and lift my bottle of Grey Goose to her red lips. Her black jeans are tight and sculpt her thick thighs and hips perfectly. My eyes follow the rest of her body towards her face; her breasts are being pushed up by a tan corset thing and her blonde hair is hanging behind her shoulders in big, loose curls. "I'm sorry about Ronan," she whispers and I nod, not sure what to say to that. Yeah, I'm fucking sorry too. If only being sorry could bring him back. "Just take it day by day. I'm here if you need anything."

I finally bring my eyes to hers. Her beautiful mint eyes glitter in the dim overhead light. "When does it get easier?"

She takes another drink from the bottle and hands it to me. I take a slow shot, finishing the bottle, and watch her throat swallow. "Everyone says the first year without someone is the hardest, but really it's the second because while everyone else has moved on, you're still living without him."

I lick my lower lip and then pull it between my teeth in thought. Allie watches my lips in rapture. "Well, that's fucking depressing." She nods, still staring at my mouth, and I get an idea. "I think I do need something from you."

Her eyes snap to mine, her brows raised. "What?"

Leaning forward, I keep my eyes on hers and run a hand up her jean-clad thigh. "You."

"Saint," she lightly protests, her eyes falling down to follow my hand's slow path up her leg and then back to my face.

My hand reaches her waist. "I know you want me."

Allie shakes her head. "But you're grieving."

My fingers press into her skin and guide her to stand in front of me. "Make me forget, Allie." I gently pull her down into my lap and she complies, sitting down and resting her hands on my shoulders. I need this. To forget about the shit that's been going on for the last few weeks. Having to bury a man that was my role model. My best friend, brother, father figure—-he'd kill me for that one—and a club brother all in one. Putting him in the ground and saying goodbye to him was the hardest thing I've ever had to do, and I know I could lose myself in Allie.

I've already been doing that for months. Any time things got hard, it was always her I went to. Thinking of her, texting her, I even stooped to cyberstalking her social medias. She's been my little secret escape.

I never crossed the line though, even though I know we've both wanted me to. She's Reese's best friend, but more than that, I knew she would consume me and I'd be fucked. Everything I did would be for her, because of her. Every thought I had. My entire world would revolve around her, and for someone who's never cared about anyone else but my club, that shit is pretty fucking scary.

To lose the one thing I had: control.

But right now I'm drowning, and I don't care if I die inside of her hurricane.

Allie leans into me. "Okay," she whispers, her breath fanning over my lips.

I don't waste any time, and I don't give her a chance to second guess herself. I bury my hand in her hair and bring her face to mine. I devour her mouth like it'll give me life, and right now it is. Her lips ease my pain and take away the grief. For one perfect moment, I haven't lost the most important person in my life. No, right now I'm kissing Allison Lenkov again. The sassy little law student who hasn't left my mind since I met her in Johnson and Hunt's law office. One of the only people who doesn't put up with my shit and puts me in my place. She's not afraid of me, she just takes me as I am.

She's still just as perfect as the first time I kissed her. If you can even call the small peck she gave me when I drove her home from Finn and Huntley's wedding a kiss. She opens her mouth for me and I dive in, taking everything I can from her. I want everything she'll give me, and then I'll take more. Her body melts into mine and that's when I know that I have her.

She's mine.

The empty vodka bottle clatters to the floor and both of my hands wrap under her ass and lift us from the chair. I lay her on the table in front of me and flick the button off her jeans. I peel the skin-tight jeans down over her ass but Allie stops me by putting her heel against my chest.

Louboutins and leather. The perfect depiction of us.

"My shoes, Saint." Her sweet, meek voice wraps around my heart and squeezes it.

I look down at her tan heels and the buckles on her ankle. "Ugh!" I groan loudly and work the tiny buckles, then toss the heels over my shoulder. They make a thunk on the hardwood floor, but it's drowned out by the song "Hurts So Good" by Astrid S leaking through the bottom of the Chapel door.

Sliding her jeans the rest of the way down, I drop them to the floor next to me and stare down at her half-naked body. She's a fucking dream, and trust me, I've dreamt of this.

"Saint," she groans, wrapping her legs around my waist and pulling me into the table. Her cheeks flame a bright red, and I love that my attention on her body causes her to blush.

My fingers wrap around her ankles and raise them to rest on my shoulders. "Say it again."

Allie bites her red bottom lip. "Say what?" she innocently asks. Bending down, I lean into her center and run my tongue from her opening up to her clit and take it between my teeth. "Saint!" she moans.

Grinning, I suck her clit into my mouth and move my hands up her sides and to the cups of her corset top, yanking them down to free her heavy tits. Then I bring a hand back down to where my mouth is. Sliding two fingers into her, her pussy squeezes me, and I pump into her, continuing to work her clit with my tongue.

Allie squeezes around me already. I knew she was going to be perfect, I just knew it. I've dreamt of this—of her—and she's magnificent.

Pulling away, I stand up and undo my jeans, sliding them down and palming my cock, running my hand up the length. "Sorry, baby, but I'm pretty sure this feeling won't go away until I'm buried deep inside of you." With that, I slam into her, not giving her a chance to answer back. Her back arches and one hand flies to my tee shirt, pulling me down to her chest. Her nails dig into my shoulder while the other hand tangles into my hair and holds me to her. I wrap my arms around her too, holding on to her with everything that I have. I won't let this woman go for anything—not now, and not ever. Not since I've had a taste of her now. Her legs fall to my waist and circle around me, locking behind my back. I bury myself as deeply as I can, but it's not enough, I need more. I shove my pants down to my ankles and step out of them, shoving my shoes off as well, and climb onto the table with her. Hovering over her and spreading her legs wide, I hold her at the back of her knees. She watches me, her light green eyes staring into my soul and holding me, anchoring me to this moment. Her eyes wrap me in a safety blanket and protect me from the grief. She's everything I've ever needed, and I knew that a while ago. I just didn't know how to get her. I rut into her so deep, branding myself into her body for the rest of her life. No other man will ever know her like this, like I do. No other man will ever have her again.

I roughly circle her clit with my thumb and work her higher, higher, and higher until she's screaming my name, her nails trying to dig into the wooden table.

"You. Are. Mine. Now." I punctuate the words with a thrust, slamming into her until I'm balls deep and spilling my cum into her.

Fuck, I didn't use a condom. I can't find a fuck to give right now, though.

Allie stands from the table, redresses, and walks to the wall, pulling a tube of lipstick from her small purse and slowly swiping it over her lips as she looks into a large mirror with the Outlaws skull printed onto it. I pull my jeans back on and slip into my shoes. Regret crashes into me. Not for what we did—I won't ever regret Allie—but because she deserves better than me, than this. I know this can't turn into anything right now, as much as I want it to. As much as I *need* it to.

"I can't be with you right now, Allie. I need to figure out who killed Ronan. I can't be the man that you deserve until I've done that. I can't give you what you need." Sitting back down in my chair, I stare at the wall in front of me, not daring to turn around and look at her. I'll break if I do; give in and put her back on this table and underneath me.

"You shouldn't shut out the people who care about you when you're grieving. Please let me help you." Her voice is soft, and it kills me.

God, I need a fucking drink. "I don't have enough to give you right now. If we're going to start something, you deserve for it to be whole and pure."

"So once you find who murdered Ronan, you'll let me in?" *Murdered.* I hate that word.

Shaking my head, I drag my hand down my face. "I don't know. I don't know the person that's going to come out on the other side of this." My voice cracks with emotion, but I push through. I have to save her before I destroy her.

"Don't lose yourself to this, Saint," she begs.

A tear runs down my face and I swipe it away before she can see. "I'll try, my Queen."

"Promise me." Allie's voice is stronger, demanding, and right behind me.

I bolt to my feet and turn around to face her, grabbing her wrist and pulling her into me. Her bag falls to the floor, but she holds her head high and keeps my stare, emotion clear in her eyes. "I can't," I whisper.

"Do it for me." She doesn't give up, and her voice doesn't falter. I nod, not being able to say anything more, and drop her wrist. She bends down and picks up her bag. "I'll wait for you, Saint," Allie says before she walks to the door of the Chapel and lets herself out.

"Please," I whisper when the door closes.

Looking down, I notice a black, cubed tube of lipstick, the gold trimming gleaming in the overhead light. Picking it up, I pull off the cap and see the bright red that Allie was wearing tonight. I snap the lid back on and slide it into my jeans pocket, slouch down into my old chair, kick my feet onto the table, and close my eyes.

2

———

ALLIE

THE DOOR CLICKS CLOSED BEHIND ME AND I LEAN AGAINST IT, THE music of the party still beating loudly around me. Closing my eyes, I rest my head against the thick wood door. I knew Saint and I were inevitable. Things were too hot between us to only ever sizzle; we were meant to burn. Maybe we'd burn each other, I don't know. I didn't expect it to end right after it began, though. I meant it when I said I'd wait for him. I'd wait for Saint Viotto forever. I *have* been waiting for Saint Viotto forever, but he's Saint, and nothing with him has ever been easy.

SEVEN MONTHS AGO...

Stepping into the small coffee shop, I pull off my leather gloves and slide them into the pocket of my wool coat. The shop is empty, except for a few people working on laptops at tables and sipping on their drinks.

"Hi." I smile at the barista behind the counter. "Medium vanilla latte with oat milk and two shots, please." She nods her head and puts my order in after taking my name. I pay and step to the side to wait.

The bell above the door jingles and a cold gust of wind rushes in

13

with the new customer. I keep my eyes cast down on my phone, but I see white Nike Air Force Ones out of the top of my vision.

"Large coffee, black. Thank you," a rough voice clips.

I roll my eyes to myself. He was a little rude. He steps up next to me to wait for his coffee, his strong, smoky cologne sliding into my nose and drowning out the coffee smell. It's intoxicating.

"Allie!" the barista calls my name, setting my cup on a small table.

Raising my head from my phone, I say, "You could have been nicer to the barista."

"Excuse me?" he snaps, and I turn my head to look at him.

I stop in my tracks, my words forgotten when I see him. Blonde hair pulled back into a bun at the back of his head, ice blue eyes, and matching blonde scruff covering his jaw. His strong brows pull together in a scowl that does nothing to diminish his beauty. Perfect teeth and plump lips. He's handsome. "Uhh," I stammer, trying to remember what I was saying. Oh right, the barista. "You could be kinder." Then I turn before he smarts off with something, and walk to the table to retrieve my coffee.

PRESENT...

Pushing off of the door, my eyes open onto the other most attractive man that I've ever met. The only man that could ever rival Saint. Mason stands on the bottom step, diagonal from me. His arms are crossed, his shoulder leans against the wall, and the hood of his hoodie sits on top of his head. His green-blue eyes are watching me, his brown hair hanging in his eyes and the light dusting of hair over his top lip makes him look like the biker that he just recently became.

I look away, purse my lips, and walk past him. I just want to go home. His hand whips out and grabs my upper arm, halting me. He jogs around to stand in front of me and leans down to look into my eyes.

"Are you okay?" he asks quietly, his dark brows lowered. He searches my face before glancing at the Chapel doors and then back again.

I grab his wrist to pull it off of my arm, and tingles zip through my hand and up my arm. The warmth of his skin flows through me and settles into my stomach. "I'm fine, Mason," I say gently.

He grabs my hand with his other and drops his hand from my arm. Holding my hand in his, he asks, "Let's get out of here."

I pull away from him. "I'm not going home with you, Mason."

He smirks, his white teeth flashing. "I wasn't offering me, Blondie, I was offering a drink." My eyes narrow on him. "Best apple martini in town, and the view is pretty fucking killer too."

I shouldn't go. I should go home. But I'm intrigued; Mason has always been at the back of my mind, always sharing glances with me. Nodding my head once, he doesn't waste any more time and pulls me through the packed clubhouse and out of the front door.

The warm July air hits my bare arms that are wrapped around Mason's body. His bike roars down the dark road.

He finally pulls into a busy, dark, gravel parking lot and pulls to a stop by the small side door. I step off and watch Mason kick the kickstand down on his black bike and turn the handlebars, shutting the engine off and swinging his leg over. He grabs my hand again and pulls me through the door. We enter into a dark hallway, the soft music of the restaurant or bar, or wherever we are, drifting into the short hallway. Light at the end spurs us forward and we step into a packed dining area; round tables with people around them, laughing over small appetizers and drinks. Mason continues pulling me toward the large bar where he leans over and motions to the bartender.

"Two apple martinis on the deck, Todd." Mason smiles and

the bartender nods, pulling the glasses from behind the bar and getting started. "Thanks!" Mason yells and grabs my hand again, pulling me towards the wall-to-wall, floor-to-ceiling windows with two large doors opening onto the deck.

We find a table against the railing and take a seat. The restaurant is sitting above a giant lake, with a mountain on the other side. Lights hang on the wooden pillar and beams of the deck, and the moon reflects off of the water below us.

"This is beautiful," I say, still looking out over the water.

"Yeah, looks even better tonight," Mason says. The last part was under his breath, but I still hear it.

Our drinks are delivered with menu books, and we flip through them.

"Do you want to share the crab cakes?" I ask, turning the page and scanning the menu.

Mason laughs. "You're sharing your food with me already? I'm flattered."

I roll my eyes. "Shut up, it's just food."

The waitress comes, calls Mason by name, and takes our order.

"You come here a lot?" I ask him, watching him lounge in the padded chair, his hood hanging around his neck, and his tan skin glowing under the warm lights.

"The burgers are good, the drinks are great, and it's quiet. It's a nice change from the clubhouse."

"Yeah, I bet. It's always a party there isn't it?" I lick the apple off of my lips and Mason's eyes bore into mine.

After a pause, he answers, "Yeah, a bit," he chuckles, then looks out over the water. His smile falls.

"I'm sorry about your President." I lean forward and rest my hand on his on the table.

Mason turns to me, his brows pulling in. "Saint?"

Shaking my head softly, I purse my lips. "Your previous President."

He nods slowly, his eyes sad. "Thanks. Wasn't much of a party tonight for Saint's promotion. We're all still trying to figure this shit out, but it's tradition to throw a party." He picks up his glass and downs the rest of the apple martini. "Do you wanna take a walk?"

Mason stands and tosses money onto the table. "A walk? Where?"

He tilts his head toward the water. "The beach." He holds out his hand and I take it, letting him lead me across the deck and down the steps at the end.

On the last step, he stops and bends down, his knees hitting the sand. "What are you doing?" I ask. The moonlight is the only light down here.

"Taking off your heels for you," he says as his hands land on my ankle and his fingers start to work the buckle. I hold onto the wood railing to steady myself and step out of my shoes as he frees my feet.

He keeps my heels in one hand and offers me the other. We walk across the sand and down to the water. Mason picks up a few small rocks and skips them across the water, the rock hitting a few times before sinking below. The muscles in his arms flex as he tosses the slim rocks. The light chatter from the restaurant above drifts down to us, but there isn't anyone else down here. He bends down again to pick up rocks, and the silence between us is comfortable. I look up at the mountain; it looks even larger from down here. Mason's body blocks my view and I look into his eyes.

"Here, I found this and thought you might like it." He holds out his hand.

Sitting in his palm is a small, teal seashell. I pick it up and bring it closer to my eyes to examine it. "It's the same color as your eyes." I turn the shell over and examine the other side.

"Really?" he asks, lifting the shell to look at it too.

I shrug, looking into his eyes and then back to the shell. "Close. Your eyes are a little greener."

His mouth kicks up in the corner. "I didn't realize you've been looking at my eyes."

Rolling my eyes, I bite the edge of my lip and pull my hand away, slipping the shell into my bag. "Don't flatter yourself."

"In My Veins" by Andrew Belle and Erin Mccarley plays on the speakers on the deck above us.

"Do you wanna dance?" Mason asks, setting my shoes on the sand.

I look at him and then at the water beside us. Setting my bag on the sand next to my shoes, I grab his hand and he pulls me into him. My arms reach up to wrap around his neck and his wrap around me, both hands resting on my hips.

We sway back and forth, listening to the music and the quiet of the night. I lean in closer to him and rest my head on his chest. His hands move from my waist, one to my lower back and the other behind my head, massaging circles on my scalp. Being in Mason's arms evokes something in me that I didn't know I had. Some warm, protected feeling.

Loved.

Adored.

He makes me feel like I'm a precious piece of art. Or some woman that needs protecting and he's here to save me. Some sappy shit like that. I don't know, I've never felt this way with anyone. All of my relationships have always felt surface-level, transactional. I need someone to be there when I need them and gone when I don't, never spending more time than necessary.

Mason's warmth floods me and I feel like I'm sitting in front of a fire with a warm blanket wrapped around me. They say there are moments that you'll look back on and know your life changed. I think this is one of those moments.

I never want this moment to end. I want to live here forever. In Mason's arms.

Mason's hands move and he slightly pulls away. He captures my cheeks in his hands and lifts my face to his. Leaning down, he softly presses his lips to mine and I melt into him without thought. My mouth opens and he slips his tongue inside, twirling with mine, but then he pulls away as quickly as he enters. He kisses my forehead and pulls me back into him.

"Sorry, I should have asked," he whispers into my hair. My arms drop to his waist and I pull him closer to me, resting my cheek on his chest again.

What did I just do? I told Saint I would wait for him and now I'm kissing his brother and liking it. No.

Loving it.

Mason is different from Saint. So different. Where Saint demands and takes, Mason is gentle and thoughtful. If I had met Mason first, if I hadn't already fallen for Saint, I'd be pushing Mason to finish what he started, to take him back to my house, to... to do what Saint and I did tonight.

Oh my god...

The song ends and I pull away from Mason. "Can you take me back to my car at the clubhouse?" I ask, looking into his sweet green eyes.

"Of course, Blondie. Let's go grab our crab cakes and go." Mason bends down to pick up my shoes and bag, offering me his arm to hold onto as we walk across the sand and back to the steps.

Mason takes my hand and leads me to sit on the steps while he kneels again and sweeps the sand off of my feet, placing my shoes back on and buckling them at my ankles. I take my bag from him and start up the stairs with Mason behind me.

Every touch, every gesture feels like a stab of a knife to my heart. I feel guilty for what I did tonight. For taking my clothes off for Saint and then kissing Mason. I feel like I'm leading one of them on, or both of them, and I don't want to. I'm realizing as time goes on that I've had a slight crush on Mason since I met him at Sophie's birthday party, the night that Reese was drugged. That's why I agreed to come with him tonight. I wanted to see what he was like when he wasn't surrounded by people. I just never thought anything would happen between us, because of Saint.

Mason stops the bike and lets me off. I watch as he backs up the bike into the row of bikes along the clubhouse. He steps off and takes my hand, leading me to my car. Once there, he opens the door for me.

"I'm sorry for that kiss, Allie." He looks ashamed and I can't have him thinking that I didn't want it. That I don't want it again.

I reach up with one hand and cup his cheek. His smooth skin feels like velvet under my hand. Leaning onto my toes, I place a kiss on his plush lips. Then another, and another. "Goodnight, Mason," I say when I finally pull away.

His smile is the brightest I've ever seen. His white teeth flash against the moonlight. "So I'll see you again then?"

I shrug and slide into my car. "I hope so."

Mason shuts my car door and I leave the clubhouse parking lot and head home.

What the fuck am I going to do?

3

______

ALLIE

WAKING UP THE NEXT MORNING, I ROLL OUT OF BED AND WALK into the kitchen, putting a pod in the Nespresso and placing a mug under the spout. Staring out of the kitchen window, my mind wanders...

SEVEN MONTHS AGO...

The soft tapping of keyboards and the light fragrance of the office greet me as I open the door. Hanging my coat on the coat stand behind my desk, I sit down and pull my laptop out of my bag.

"What's my schedule today, Ms. Lenkov?" Mr. Johnson asks as he walks by my desk and into his office.

Picking up the iPad, I follow him into his office and take a seat in front of his large, walnut desk. "You have a 9 A.M. with S. Viotto, lunch at 11, court at 1, and Partners meeting at 4. Paralegals have everything prepared for court."

Mr. Johnson finishes pulling everything out of his briefcase and looks up at me, smiling. "Thank you, Allie."

"Anything else?" I ask.

He shakes his head. "Nope, just send in Mr. Viotto when he gets here." Nodding once, I stand up and leave his office, returning to my desk.

I hear the door open a while later and the rush of cold air floats in. Picking my head up, I see the rude man from the coffee shop. He saunters through the office, passing the desks of the paralegals, and stops between mine and Ainsley's desk, the other law assistant. My eyes follow him the entire way, and his smirk is plastered on his face as he watches me back.

We stare at each other, neither of us saying a word, but when Ainsley clears her throat, his eyes pull away from me and to her.

"Can I help you?" Ainsley purrs. I internally roll my eyes. Not him, babe.

The man's eyes come back to me and he points to the door behind me, Mr. Johnson's office.

"Mr. Viotto?" I ask, standing.

His eyes fall down my body and back up. My face heats but I clear my throat to cover it, turning around to let Mr. Johnson know his appointment is here.

"It's Saint, please." His deep voice ghosts over my neck behind me.

I quickly turn around, and he's right there, staring down at me with intense eyes. "What?" I ask, breathless.

"You can call me Saint." His lips slide into a small smile. His pink, plump lips are soft despite the frigid weather outside.

"That's a different name," I say the first thing that comes to mind.

He shrugs with one shoulder and steps around me, opening the door without a knock and closing it behind him.

PRESENT...

"Will you make me one?" Sophie yawns, shuffling into the kitchen in her sleep shirt and shorts.

I shake my head, leaving the memory of Saint behind, and reach for another mug from the cabinet. "Always stealing my coffee." I set the steaming mug in front of her when the machine stops dripping.

"You're the best at making it." She smiles over the white mug. I sit down across from her at our high-top kitchen table, bringing my coffee with me. "You got in late last night." She watches me while we both take drinks from our cups.

"I went to an Outlaw party," I say, my mind still reeling from last night.

"Oh." Sophie's eyebrows raise. "How was that? You seem off." Her eyes narrow. She's always been great at reading people, and right now she's using it on me.

Biting my lip, I think about what I want to say, and how I want to say it. "I don't know. I've liked one of the members for a while now, and last night we escalated whatever we have to another level. Then when I was still vulnerable from that, another member invited me out for drinks and I went. I found out I like him too."

"Why did you go out for drinks if you like the first guy?" Sophie hedges.

I shake my head. Why did I go? "Curiosity, I think? I don't know, really. I wasn't thinking, I just wanted to go, so I did."

"Okay, so you like them both. What's the issue? Why do you look so fucking glum?" Soph takes another sip.

I blink my eyes rapidly, trying to wake up and figure out where the confusion is for her. "That I like them both," I snap.

Soph rolls her eyes. Typical. "Has either asked you to be exclusive or asked you out?"

"No," I answer slowly.

"Then fucking relax and just see where it goes. Enjoy two hot men chasing you before your ass settles with a hedge fund manager or developer and moves to Seattle or New York."

Turning my head, I look out of the kitchen window and

watch the trees in the backyard. "I don't think it's going to be that easy."

Sophie walks to the sink and dumps the remainder of her coffee. "You're the one with the vag, make it that easy." I watch her rinse her mug and then put it in the dishwasher.

"I told Saint that I would wait for him though, and then I went on a date with Mason." I bury my head in my hands. It feels even worse in the daylight.

Sophie leans against the counter, watching me. "You can't wait on someone forever, Al. You'll look up and you're eighty and lived your entire life waiting for something that never happened. Letting everything that could have made you happy pass you by while you wait for someone who isn't waiting for you." She pushes off and walks towards me. "Don't do that to yourself. Don't waste your life."

She places a soft kiss on my head as she walks past me and into the hallway.

I guess there isn't any harm in getting to know Mason. Saint didn't promise me anything, not even the hope of something when he was done with his vengeance mission.

4

SAINT

BANG, BANG, BANG! LEO POUNDS A MALLET ON A FENDER, WORKING out a dent in the open garage bay of Evans Body Shop. He's sitting on a short rolling chair, bobbing his head to "Let You Go" by Machine Gun Kelly. Walking by, I shove his stool with my foot, sending him rolling a few feet away.

"Hey, asshole," Leo chuckles, rolling back to where he was working.

I throw up two fingers in greeting as I walk to the door to the office. Finn is sitting behind the desk, his hat backward and wearing an old black tee shirt.

I step inside and sit down in one of the chairs across from him. "Didn't you hire your wife so that you could be the one working in the shop?" I stare at him, leaning back in the seat and eating a burrito.

"I'm just eating breakfast. Huntley said she had to stop to get Noctem a pup cup," he chuckles, taking another bite of his food.

I nod, my eyes moving around the office. It's only been a few weeks since Huntley started, but she's already transformed this office into something professional and nice. It used to be plain white walls, a desk, chairs, and a mini fridge. Now the back wall is painted a deep green with two long, floating shelves and a large, potted plant in the corner. Pictures of Finn and Huntley at their wedding and on their honeymoon with Noctem are framed and sitting on the shelves, as well as Huntley's and Finn's diplomas and certifications. "I need you to sell something for me," I say, finally looking back at him.

He leans back in the chair further, his hands resting behind his head. "Sell what?"

"56 K-Model. Half restored."

Finn cocks one eyebrow. "I could probably find someone for that." I nod. "I didn't know you were collecting," he continues.

Sighing, I rub my eyes before answering. "Ro was helping me fix it up, but I usually just sat and talked to him while he worked. I never did anything so I can't finish it."

"You got a picture?" Finn leans forward. I pull my phone out of my pocket and scroll through my pictures, finding the latest. Clicking the photo, I hold my phone out to him and he takes it, looking over it. "This is nice." His thumb and index finger pinch in on the photo and then he moves it around. "I could finish it up for you. You can come in and annoy me, or bitch, or whatever you would do with Ro." Finn smiles, and it *almost* reaches his eyes.

"What about Huntley?" I ask.

He shrugs one shoulder. "She might join us some nights."

I roll my eyes. "I guess." I smile so he knows I'm joking.

Nails rapidly tap against the concrete floor of the shop and a black ball of fur flies into the office, clearing the side of the chair and jumping right into Finn's lap. Noctem's front paws rest on Finn's chest as she licks his face and neck. Huntley walks into the office a few moments later, carrying a coffee cup and a bag of food.

"I thought Noctem needed whipped cream?" I ask.

Huntley smiles and sits down next to me. "She said I could

get coffee and a sandwich. Want Finn's cake pop?" She smiles at me, so much brighter than she used to be.

"No, thank you." I shake my head, turning back to Finn. "I'll have Nox drop the bike off. Let me know when you start on it."

"Come by tomorrow, Prez. We can start then," he says.

Shaking my head, I think about that name. "Still doesn't feel real," I say softly.

Finn looks down at the desk, twirling a pen around with his finger. "None of it does."

"Alright, just text me." I stand up and walk to the door, leaving the shop and taking my bike back to SIN.

5

MASON

Groaning, I rub my eyes and roll over in my bed to grab my phone off of the small table next to it. I slide the screen unlocked and the faceID scans my tired, half-closed eyes and opens onto my home screen. Clicking on Instagram, I pull up Allie's profile, just like every morning, and see if she's posted anything new. She hasn't, so I scroll through her old photos that I've seen so many times before. Pictures of her coffee orders, food, flowers, and pictures of her and her friends with the same filter on every picture.

Tossing my phone onto the pillow beside me, I get up, get dressed in a cut-off shirt and shorts, grab my phone and my gym bag, and walk out of my room at the clubhouse to go to the gym.

After showering, I land in my seat in front of my computer with a protein shake, shaking it while my systems turn on.

The two screens in front of me slowly light up, and I lean my head back against the chair. All I've been able to think about is Allie and finally kissing her last night. I've been stealing glances of her since I first saw her at that fucking fail of a birthday party that Wyatt and I took the Princess to. She was swaying her hips, her black dress hugging her body, and her shiny blonde hair brushing across her shoulders and upper back. A fucking dream if I've ever seen one. She held me captive the entire time she danced on the dance floor with her friends, and then last night... Her tight black jeans, her red lips. *Fuck.* Her arms wrapped around me on my bike, then holding onto my shoulders on the beach. I could have died then and been the happiest man in the world. I've been waiting for some sign from her, something to let me know she wanted me to make a move, but last night as she leaned against the Chapel doors, her eyes conflicted and body closed off, I had to say something. I had to get her out of there.

Best decision of my entire life.

Typing in my passwords, I pull up my tracking system and type in Allie's phone number. The ping's color radiates as it loads and then pops up on a map, showing Allie at work, since she's on summer break right now from school. Erasing her number, I type in Saint's and wait for his to load. I track all of the club members every morning to make sure everyone is safe, but mostly to keep up on my skills, kind of like a little test every morning. I started adding Allie to the list a while ago, telling myself it was just another level to the test, but I also wanted to make sure she was okay. Saint is at his tattoo shop, so I go through the rest of the members, even throwing Red in at the end. Once I've checked everyone's locations, I plug in Ronan's phone and start working on it from the night of his murder two weeks ago.

Murder.

Two weeks.

I've been around death, of course I have. But one of us being murdered? That's not something I thought I would experience. I kind of thought we were larger than life. Invincible. How fucking moronic that was, but I did. Until now, we'd been the ones in front of everyone. A step ahead of anyone who had it out for us. Even Reese's stalker, we were able to stop, a little later than we'd have liked, but we did it.

But this... For someone to have murdered not only a brother, but our President? All of us are processing this differently. Saint's shut the fuck down, a little more irritable than usual, and a lot more closed off. He's hurting badly, and I feel for him. Cale and Finn are holding onto each other and their women and trying to keep Saint from eating a bullet. Leo and Jack are a lot like me, confused, and concerned for themselves as well as the club. The oldies are broken, grieving. Wyatt's taking it pretty hard, he was close to Ro, too. He's talked about transferring to another chapter, getting out of Washington and leaving it all behind. I'd hate to see him go, but I understand his need to distance himself.

Saint ordered me to do whatever I could to figure out why Ro was in that alley. What he was doing by the docks. It's a shady part of town and we don't have any business down there. Was this a hit or random? What the fuck happened? The police say it was a mugging, but who mugs the President of the Devil's Outlaws? It just doesn't make any sense.

Getting started, I check all of the cell phones that pinged in the area at the time of the murder. It takes hours to sift through all of the phones that were around the docks, but nothing is suspicious. There is one camera that looks into the alley, and I wipe it clean before ever watching what is on it. I don't need to see it, I know what happened in that alley.

I pull up Ronan's texts again and start looking through them, making sure I didn't miss anything the last two times I went through them.

6

_____

SAINT

KNOCK, KNOCK. MY KNUCKLES RAP ON THE DOORFRAME OF NOX'S room—my old room. The door is open and he's standing on a chair, hanging a Harley poster on the wall above his desk.

"Hey, Prez." He smiles at me, hands still raised tacking the poster in place.

I walk in and take a seat on his bed, opposite the desk. "I just wanted to check and see how you're settling in." I look around his room. It's still a little empty, but that's normal for the Prospects. His dresser is sitting against the wall by the bathroom door, his desk is filled with energy drink cans and his laptop, and his bedside table has a small lamp on it. The only other things in the room are his bed and the chair he's standing on. His cut is laying on the bed next to me. The leather is brand new and dark black, and the Prospect patch on the back is bright white. "I know we kind of threw you into shit really quickly, then you moved into the clubhouse, and then..." I trail off, not able to say his name.

Nox hops off of the chair and sits on it backward, his arms resting on the back of it as he watches me. "Yeah, it's been," he takes a deep breath, his finger running over his chin. "Pretty fucking intense this last month, but I guess I signed up for this though, right?"

I look around the room again, I don't like this shit. The feelings, the talking. I shouldn't have taken the gavel, this isn't me. "We all signed up for it, but I don't think any of us ever thought it would happen."

"I thought he was larger than life," he whispers.

A silent laugh escapes me. "He always seemed that way, even when he was just a brand new President."

"How did you meet him?" Nox asks, resting his chin on his fist.

Biting my lip, I lean forward and rest my elbows on my knees and think back to when I first met Ronan. "I was a sophomore in college, pre-med, and I was working part-time at the hospital. He came in with a stab wound after he got into a fight at Mickey's. His black hair was longer then, sticking up in every direction, and even with a knife sticking out of his stomach, he still had his dopey fucking smile on his face." I laugh at the memory, feeling like he's right here with me. "I checked him in and since the doctor was a friend of my father's and he pulled some strings, I was able to go back and observe. Ronan and I talked the entire time and a week later I dropped out of school, quit my job, and was prospecting for the club. I went to EMT school in the evenings so I could patch guys up or help until we made it to a hospital. It's how I earned my top rocker."

Nox's eyebrows raise. "You were in medical school?"

Licking my lips, I answer, "Almost. My dad's Chief of Surgery at the biggest hospital in Seattle, so it's the family legacy."

"Oh, shit." Nox releases a breath and then laughs. "That's why they call you Dr. Viotto?"

I roll my eyes. "Yeah. I'm not sure if it's a dig for dropping out of school or because I'm the club 'doctor.'"

Nox nods his head, then his eyebrows pull together. "Wait, so you haven't been in the club long then?"

Shaking my head, I look out of the door and into the hallway, watching Mason walk by, his face buried in his phone. "No, I joined when I was twenty, became VP two years ago when our last VP moved chapters. Ro had only been President for three years at the time, and there were guys with more seniority and higher up in the hierarchy, but Ro wanted me and everyone else thought I made a good fit so I took it." I sit up straight. "It's why Finn took VP instead of Cale, even though Cale was next in line for it. He didn't want it and turned it down so it moved to Finn. We work a little differently than other clubs."

Nox nods. "Yeah, I'm starting to see that."

"Anyways." My phone vibrates in my pocket and I pull it out, the notification saying that Allie posted a new photo on Instagram. "I just wanted to check on you and make sure that your head and your heart were still with us."

"I'm still here," Nox confirms. "I want to be a part of this club more now than ever."

"Good." I stand up and take a step toward the door, but I turn around and look at the room again. "And get something other than Harley and girl posters, don't be that stereotypical." With that, I turn around and step through the door, Nox's laughter following me out of the room.

Clicking on the notification from earlier, Allie's picture opens on my screen, a martini glass with three olives sitting on a dark bar fills my screen. *"Xoxo"* is the caption, a location tagged at the top of the picture. I roll my eyes, remembering the scene in the first season of *Gossip Girl,* when Blair is sitting at a hotel bar waiting for Serena. When Allie said that was her favorite show, I went home and watched the entire thing. No doubt she is living out her *Gossip Girl* fantasies at the Madison, a high-class hotel in the town that sits right along the Sound. A beautiful little coastal town, Orca Bay. It's only about ten minutes from Merrill Hill and the towns are basically one at this point, which is why I was able to have my residence in the little town even though our territory is Merrill Hill.

Maybe I'll drive by on my way home.

7

ALLIE

A soft instrumental song floats through the bar of the Madison. The dim lights cast everyone in a soft glow, not that many people are here on a Monday evening.

"I'll never understand why you chose this small town over New York," my dad says as he slides onto the chair next to me.

Because it was completely across the country from you, I think. "I like the charm and the nature." I mean, that's also true.

He makes a disgusted sound and signals the bartender over. I take the chance to look over him. It's only been a few weeks since I was last in New York with him, and he still looks the same, but really he hasn't changed a lot in the last twenty years. He takes very good care of himself. His black hair is starting to gray at the temples, and he's starting to get some lines at the corners of his normal blue eyes. I look nothing like him, and everything like my mom. The woman who hated my dad so much that she left me behind too. She fell in love with someone else and left, but I wish she had taken me as well.

"So why were you in town?" I ask after the bartender has set my dad's drink down.

"A client, and I thought I'd check in on you while I was

here." Since when? He completely ignored me when I was in New York a few weeks ago, only having anything to do with me when we went to the dinner he needed me to attend with him.

I hum quietly and nod my head. I'm not buying his fake concern for me, but I don't know why else he would be here.

"Are you still living with that girl in my house?" he asks, taking a sip of his drink.

"Sophie, yes. Though I think she may be getting back with her ex and she'll probably move in with him." I stare at the mirror on the back of the bar and watch the few people milling about the bar.

He nods, pretending to care. "Are you seeing anyone?" Ah, that's what this is about. He knows someone and wants to set me up with them.

"No, and I'm not looking to get into anything until after law school." That's a lie, but probably what I should do instead of chasing two bikers. Oh gosh, what have I gotten myself into?

My dad pulls his phone out of his suit pocket and checks his phone. "I have to be getting back to New York. I'll let you know when I land." *No, he won't, he never does.* He stands and tosses some bills on the countertop, covering his drink and mine.

He turns and walks away, no more of a goodbye than that. I'm used to it though, actually, if he hugged me or told me he loved me I'd check him for a fever.

I signal to the bartender and order another drink. With everything going on in my head, I need some time to just sit and think without anyone distracting me.

THREE MONTHS AGO...

"Reese said she's on her way!" Soph yells over the music, standing on the opposite side of the small round table from me. Logan holds

onto her shoulders and the moving lights of the club sparkle off of her silver dress.

"Good! It's about time she left Callum's townhouse," I say, taking the shot that someone bought for the birthday girl and her party.

Emma smacks my arm, scowling at me. "Someone broke into her house again, Allie."

Shit. That was rude. "That wasn't how I meant it, I just meant it's not good for her to be inside all of the time. I understand that she's scared."

A few minutes later, Reese walks into the bar, two tall guys walking slightly behind her. Clearly, club muscle sent to watch over her. Both brunettes, but one has some laugh lines starting to set into his handsome face—ya know, if dads are your thing—but the other... The taller of the brunettes is young, probably my age, with these interesting green eyes. A clean-shaven face and pieces of chocolate hair that hang in his eyes. Reese introduces us and he holds out his hand, veiny and strong, and stares into my eyes. His gaze is too intense, his hand too firm to be a casual hello. He's gorgeous. The hard planes of his face look sharper under the shadowy light of the club.

I notice him watching me when we head to the dance floor, and I like the attention. I like the way his eyes follow me and he doesn't care that I know he's watching. I feel treasured in his eyes, and it's spurring me on. Making me sway my hips a little more, flip my hair a little more, do everything just a little more so I can keep his attention.

"Stop undressing him with your eyes and go talk to him, Al," Reese says when we get back to our table. Mason and the other guy standing at the table behind us.

I push my hair over my shoulder, turning away from Mason. "He's very cute, but I've got my sights set a little higher." Lie. He's more than 'very cute,' he's a downright masterpiece in human flesh, and 'my sights' hasn't spoken to me in over a month. I think Saint forgot about me.

The rest of the night turns into a blur, drink after drink, shot after shot. That's why I didn't go after Reese when she ran off to the bathroom. At that point, all I could think about was the floaty feeling of the drinks and the beat of the music and how I wanted to move my body to it. There's a commotion at the front door, yelling, and bodies moving. Mason storms through the crowd, everybody parting to let him through. He marches right up to the table and grabs my arms, leaning into my face.

"Where's Reese?" God, he smells so good, and his hands feel good on my skin, warm and strong. I sway backward, my head falling back to stare into his eyes. "Allie! Where's Reese?" he yells.

Oh shit, right, he's talking. I look around, but Reese isn't here. She left for the bathroom, I remember her saying she didn't feel good. I point toward the back of the club where the bathrooms are. "She went to the bathroom." Before I've even finished my sentence, Mason is letting go of me and stalking toward the back of the club, taking his scent with him.

I lose track of Mason and the other guy in the crowd, and I don't see him again until he's practically carrying Reese out of the bar. Her arms wrapped around the guys' shoulders.

"Oh my God!" Emma breathes. "What's wrong with her?"

I shake my head, my eyes going wide. "I don't know." Worry sets in for my friend. I should have gone with her, I should have paid better attention to her. What happened to her?

Emma and I rush after Mason and Reese, but when we catch up to them outside, the other guy is carrying Reese and Mason is nowhere to be seen.

"What happened to her?" I yell, pulling on the guy's really thick arm.

A white truck speeds up to the curb next to us, slamming on the brakes. "She'll fill you in later," he bites out, opening the back door. No anger in his voice, more concern, like mine. Mason's head turns around and catches my attention from the driver's seat.

"No." I yank his arm again. "You'll tell me now."

He pulls away from me and gets into the backseat, Reese uncon-
scious in his lap. "I can't. Call Callum."

He slams the door and the truck speeds away. "I don't have his
number!" I yell after them, glaring at the taillights that are rapidly
getting smaller.

"Don't you know one of the guys in the club?" Emma asks softly
beside me.

Combing my fingers through my hair, I think about Saint.
Damnit, I didn't want to be the one to reach out again, but this is
different. This is about Reese. "Yeah, come on. Let's go call him."

Emma follows me into a side alley and leans against the wall next
to me. The alley is bright and right off of The District's main road, but
it's not as busy and loud as the main walkway.

Saint picks up after the four longest rings of my life. I was
convinced he wasn't going to answer.

"Allie, are you okay?" Saint's voice demands down the line, his
tone hard and sharp.

I swallow and glance at Emma, she's watching me intently. Of
course, she is, this isn't about me, this is about Reese. "Yeah, I'm fine.
Your goons wouldn't tell us what's wrong with Reese. They rushed
her out of Mickey's and sped off with her. She was unconscious,
Saint!"

"Cale thinks she was drugged, but we don't know that for sure. Is
anyone else from your group feeling sick?" He's calm. He's always
calm. How is he calm right now?

I look at Emma again. Looking her over, she seems completely
fine, not even drunk. "No, I think we're all fine."

"Okay, well I have to go to Cale's to figure out what happened. Get
out of the bar and go home, Allie," Saint snaps.

"Okay," I answer, pushing off of the brick wall.

He pauses for so long that I pull the phone away to check if he
hung up without saying anything. He didn't, so I put the phone back
to my ear. "I'll come over when I get done here."

"What?" I ask, but then I hear the beep that tells me this time he did hang up.

After telling everyone what happened to Reese, it really didn't take much to convince everyone to go home. Emma, Sophie, Logan, and I share a rideshare, with Emma getting dropped off first, me next, and Soph and Logan heading to his house last. At least someone's night won't be ending terribly.

Grabbing a glass of water, I sit on the couch and scroll through the delivery app, looking for something greasy. My buzz had pretty much gone away on the car ride home, and now I need food.

A bike rumbles outside, and I stand up and walk to the window beside the door, looking out onto my driveway. Saint is stepping off of his bike. Flinging the door open, I rush out onto the porch, watching him walk toward me. His eyes are narrowed and his walk measured.

He completely skips the two steps to the porch and is in front of me before I can react. He runs his hands down the mesh sleeves of my black dress. "Are you sure you're okay?"

Nodding, I lean my head back so I can look up at him. "Yeah, I'm just hungry now."

Saint chuckles and pulls away. "Get your stuff then and let's go."

Walking back inside, I grab my bag and close the door, locking it on my way out.

"How did you know where I live?" I ask, but I'm only answered with a deep laugh.

Saint takes us to a small pizza place downtown, and we walk along the raised walkway, overlooking the passing cars and the water. This is the first time I've ever spent real time with Saint. Outside of when I assisted on his case with Mr. Johnson, this is the first time I've ever been alone with Saint. His blonde hair is free, hanging above his shoulders, and brushing against his tan neck. He looks down at me, catching me staring at him and I quickly avert my eyes, embarrassed that he caught me staring. He sucks the pizza grease off of his fingers and then I feel them brush against my temple, pushing my hair *behind my ear. My eyes snap up to his, his ice-blue eyes watching me. No arrogance, no annoyance, just Saint.*

"You know I haven't stopped thinking about you since I met you in that coffee shop." He leans into me, his chest brushing my chin. "Why can't I stop thinking about you?"

PRESENT...

My phone vibrates on the table and I pick it up, a text from distraction number one.

SAINT:

Be safe getting home.

ALLIE:

How did you know I wasn't home?

SAINT:

You literally tagged your location on Instagram.

ALLIE:

I didn't know you checked on me.

SAINT:

I might have scrolled past.

SAINT:

Do you want a ride home?

I finish my drink in a gulp and stare at my phone. Of course, I want to see him. I haven't stopped thinking about him since Saturday at the party and I miss him. I want to know how he is.

ALLIE:

From you?

SAINT:

Of course. I wouldn't send a Prospect to collect you.

ALLIE:

Okay, I'm ready.

I walk to the lobby of the hotel and wait for the loud rumble of Saint's bike.

A few minutes later, a single headlight pulls up in front of the double doors and stops. My feet carry me to the door, my heels clicking on the marble floor. The doorman opens the door for me and I step through. Saint leans against his white bike. It used to be black, but I think it's a President thing; Ronan's bike was white too. His arms are crossed and his permanent scowl is sitting on his face. His blonde hair is pulled into a bun on the back of his head and his white tee shirt, light jeans, and white Air Forces are all sticking out like a sore thumb at the hotel, with men walking in with custom suits and women wearing Jimmy Choo and Alaïa, and trying not to stare at the bad boy biker sitting in front of a luxury hotel. My black bodycon dress isn't going to ride well on the back of his bike, but I'd ride that thing naked if it meant I was with him. The bike, not him... well... both actually.

His eyes follow down my body, the low neckline, tight dress, and exposed legs. "I'll ride slow," he says, reaching out a hand for me.

Taking it, he leads me to his bike and swings his leg over, keeping a hold of my hand to stabilize me as I stand on the small pegs in my favorite So Kates.

Saint pulls out of the driveway and slowly drives down the street that follows the Sound. I look out over the water, hoping I might be able to see a pod of Orcas under the moonlight, but the water is still. The mountains and islands on the other side of the

Sound are barely visible in the dark, but I watch them anyway. I love it in Orca Bay. The small town is quiet and beautiful, and the view is breathtaking. It probably wasn't the best idea to have Saint take me home. How am I going to get my car back in the morning when I have work? I lean forward to ask him when I notice that we're not headed in the direction of Merrill Hill, in fact, we're headed in the opposite direction.

"Where are you taking me?" I ask, leaning into his ear so he can hear me.

Saint turns his head slightly, yelling over the motor of the bike, "My house."

I open my mouth to say something else, but Saint revs the engine and speeds forward. I clutch his stomach, holding onto him tighter and pressing my cheek to the patches on the back of his cut. The warm summer air feels good around us, the water bringing in a little bit of chill and making the night comfortable.

Saint turns off of the main road and goes halfway up the hill of Orca Bay. He pulls into the driveway of a large home with black siding. When we're off the bike, he takes my hand and leads me to the front door. Opening the thick wood door and stepping through, his house is exactly what I expected from him. Simplistic and neutral. An office is on the left as we walk in, but he has it as a billiards room. The walls are painted black with a pool table with black velvet over top and the Devil's Outlaws logo painted in white in the middle. He walks ahead of me into the open living room and kitchen. Wall-to-wall windows over-look the Sound, a clear view with a grassy backyard in front of it. The dining room is behind the kitchen, with bay windows and a round table in the middle. A low, black sectional takes up most of the living room, a light wood table in front of it and a large TV hung on the wall. The kitchen is all light wood and black accents. Saint leans on the butcher's block kitchen island and tosses his keys into a large wooden bowl. Pulling out his phone, he types around while I walk through his house and take everything in.

"Do you want pizza?" Saint calls out to me as I get to the doors that lead to the backyard.

"Yeah," I say back, turning the knob and stepping onto the stone behind the house. There's a large open area, an outdoor kitchen to my right, and a long, rectangular gray outdoor table with about 10 plush, gray chairs around it.

Wide steps lead to a few more feet of large stone before it ends and the lush green grass starts, an open yard that looks like it drops off right into the water. Big potted plants sit at the top and bottom of the stairs. It's so beautiful out here. Turning around, I see a wrap-around deck on the second floor. I bet the view is even better up there.

"What kind of pizza do you want?" Saint yells from the patio doors. I look at where he's standing, shoulder resting against the doorframe, the light pouring in from behind him and casting a glow around him, and my breath catches in my throat. He's one of the most stunning men I've ever seen, even more so since I've come to see parts of him he doesn't show many people. Emotionally, but also physically now. The emotion he poured into me that night at the clubhouse was more than he's ever given me. He was so broken, and he still is.

"Pineapple and ham," I answer him finally, walking back toward the door.

Saint rolls his eyes and turns around, walking back into the house and to the island where he was before.

I step into the house, the warm-toned wood floors shine and my steps thunk across it. Saint's eyes rise from his phone and he watches me. His light blue gaze bares into me, burrowing deep into my soul and holding it hostage. "Water Fountain" by Alec Benjamin plays softly through the speakers in the ceiling, filling the open space with the easy, bouncy beat.

"Why did you bring me here?" I ask Saint when I get to his side at the long, wide island and he stands up straight next to me.

He swallows roughly. "I couldn't stay away." He looks down at me.

I step closer, my chest almost brushing his stomach. "You don't have to stay away."

Saint shakes his head, scrunching his eyes closed. "I can't give you what you need right now, Allie."

My face sets in a hard line. "Let me decide what I need."

"I can't give you what I need." His voice raises and he pushes away from me and walks to the large refrigerator, taking a bottle of vodka from the freezer. Grabbing a short glass from the glass front cabinet next to the fridge, he pours the vodka in and downs half the glass. Setting the glass on the counter behind him, he leans against it and watches me, still standing at the island.

"Then what can you give me?" I ask, slowly stepping toward him.

His eyes track me, his knuckles squeezing the counter behind him. When I reach him, I grab hold of his cut and pull myself into him, and I feel his stomach muscles flex at the contact before relaxing again. Staring at my lips, he answers, "Me. When I'm too lost to find my way home."

Letting out a long breath, I nod. "I can work with that."

Saint tries to pull my hands off of him, but I hold on tighter, not letting him walk away from this. "You shouldn't have to 'work with' anything, Allie."

"I'll work with you, for you, next to you, until you figure this shit out." Saint's cologne pulls me in, the spicy musk mixed with vanilla. I sway toward him, and his hands finally land on my hips. His fingers digging into my skin.

He leans down, his lips grazing my forehead when the doorbell rings.

Saint sighs and pushes off of the counter, moving my body away from him with his hands on my hips. I watch him leave the kitchen and take a deep breath. It's hard to keep my head around Saint. I always act on instinct when it comes to him; my brain shuts off and I just think with emotions. The same way I did with Mason at Saint's promotion party, I guess.

Saint returns with two large pizza boxes and a smaller box on top. He opens the oven at the end of the counter I'm standing in front of and places them in. Slamming the door closed, he turns and stalks towards me. My eyes widen a second before he's lifting me up and my legs are wrapping around his waist on instinct.

"What are you doing?" I ask as he walks us through the house and to a set of stairs with matching wood and black iron railings.

"Going home," he answers, taking the stairs and walking down a hall. The lights are off, so I can't make anything out, other than the floors are wood up here too, I can hear it in the way Saint's shoes hit the floor.

Saint shuffles me around so he can use one hand to open a door and when we step through he slams it closed. He walks through the room until he falls on top of me on a soft bed. The comforter puffs up around us and he leans into me, running his nose up the column of my neck and to my chin, where he gently bites down.

"Is this okay?" Saint rasps above me, his mouth hovering over mine.

"Yes!" I breathe, pulling him to me by his cut. His mouth attacks mine, his hands clutching me tightly.

Saint pulls away, his nose brushing over my cheek. "I need you, Al. I need you. I'm losing myself."

I grab his face between my hands and pull him back to look at me. Tears pool in his eyes and my heart shatters. "I know. I'm here," I whisper back, pulling him to my lips.

Saint rolls over, bringing me with him so I wind up straddling him while he lays on the bed. "I want to watch you." He runs his hand down my side, slowly, caressing.

Pushing off of the bed, I stand in front of it. My shins brush against the silky comforter between Saint's spread legs. I reach back and pull down the zipper of my dress, letting it fall to the floor. Saint stares at my bare chest and my black lace thong. He sits up as I step out of my heels, and he takes off his cut, handing it to me.

"What do you want me to do with that?" I ask, looking down at his outstretched hand.

"Wear it." I take it and hold the collar of it, watching Saint pull his shirt over his head and start working on his jeans. "Put it on, my Queen." He stands to push his jeans down and kick his shoes off, and I slip the worn leather over my arms. It's heavy and sits like a comforting weight on my shoulders. The leather is worn and soft, and it smells like Saint. "Only the cut," Saint says, bending down slightly to push my thong over my hips. He sits down and pulls it the rest of the way down my legs.

Stepping out of them, Saint takes them and places them in the inside pocket of his cut. Placing my hands on his shoulders, I kneel on the bed, my legs on either side of his waist and he lays back, his hands landing on my hips and lifting me up. I position him at my entrance and push down on him, letting him fill me slowly and tossing my head back with the tight feel of him. Saint and I groan in unison as I sink to the bottom of his shaft. He holds me under the cut, his warm hands burning into my skin and rushing through my veins. He directs me over him, moving me exactly as he wants, his teeth biting into his bottom lip.

"Fuck, Allie," Saint hisses, his fingertips digging into my hips, rocking me faster.

Tossing my head back, I moan, "Saint, I'm close."

With a lift of his hips, Saint lifts me off of him and positions me on the bed on my stomach, pulling out of me and a whimper falls from my lips. I was about to cum. He bends down and kisses my ass cheek before slapping it hard.

I yelp and he massages the tender flesh before pushing back inside of me again. Grabbing his forearms, I dig my nails into the skin, creating little crescents with my manicured nails. I arch my back so he can slide in further and he follows me by pumping into me harder, losing himself in the motions behind me.

"Roll me over, I want to hold you when you cum," I moan, laying my forehead on the silky black comforter.

Saint pulls out of me again and I turn over. He's on me before I can pull him to me, sliding back in and looking into my eyes. He's unfocused, not himself, and I grab his face with both hands and make him look at me.

Saint lowers himself onto one arm and comes closer, our chests brushing as he thrusts into me. With the other hand, he reaches between us and circles my clit in time with his hips moving against mine.

"I'm here, Saint. We're here together," I whisper into his lips. "I'm here, Saint, I'm here," I chant. His hips pick up speed with my words. "Oh God, I'm cumming!" I throw my head back against the bed and Saint's mouth suctions to my neck, biting and sucking while I feel his warm cum spill into me.

Saint whispers something against my throat, but before I can ask what he said, he pulls out of me and walks through a set of double doors and into an attached bathroom.

Laying there, I look around his room. Wall-to-wall windows line the wall next to the bed, much like downstairs, black walls, a warm wood headboard and matching dresser against the wall at the end of the bed, and a large, fluffy, black rug that takes up the majority of the room. There is one plush, tan chair with a matching ottoman in the corner of the room by the windows with a large, black, leather case leaning against it.

Saint steps into the room, his bare feet softly slapping against the wood. His long, lean legs have a few tattoos scattered on his thighs, and he has two full sleeves on his arms. It hits me that this is the first time I've seen him naked. Last time we had sex he didn't even take off his shirt, only his jeans, and I wasn't really paying attention to his legs when he was fucking me into the table. I've seen his arms when he's worn short sleeve shirts, but that's it. The bed dips as he kneels next to me and places a warm washcloth on my inner thighs, gently cleaning me up. I watch him wipe at me and when he stands and walks back to the bathroom, his back has the patches that are on his cut tattooed across his shoulders and then his lower back, and the skull with the snakes is outlined and parts filled in like he hasn't had it finished yet. When it's done it'll look identical to his cut.

Saint comes back a few seconds later, leaving the washcloth in the bathroom and coming to the bed, he leans down and speaks next to me. "Lay down. I'll warm up the pizza and bring it up." And I watch him grab a pair of gray sweatpants from the dresser along the wall, pull them on, and walk out of the bedroom.

I don't feel right eating in his bed, so I get up and pick my dress up, walk over, and lay Saint's cut on the arm of the chair in the corner. Pulling on my dress, I walk out of Saint's giant bedroom and walk down the stairs and into the living area. Saint turns around at the sound of my bare feet hitting the wooden steps, a ghost of a smile on his face.

Ignoring him, I walk to the table and take the seat with my back to him so I can stare out at the water.

Saint carries over two plates with pizza on them, setting one down in front of me and the other across the table from me. Turning around, he walks back to the kitchen and returns a few seconds later with a glass of wine and a short tumbler of clear liquid. He sets the wine glass down in front of me and places a gentle kiss on my temple as he does so.

I watch him in awe as he goes to his seat. He's so gentle with me tonight. I like it, but I also like when he's snappy with me. When he challenges me and pushes my buttons. I just like him. A lot.

8

ALLIE

THE FIRST RAYS OF THE MORNING SUN STREAM IN THROUGH THE wall of windows, so I roll over and reach out for Saint, but where he slept last night is cold and empty, and my hand glides over the black, silk sheets. I snap my eyes open and look around the room for him. Finally, I turn back over and face the windows. Saint is sitting in the tan armchair, shirtless, with his bare feet propped up on the ottoman, his knees bent, and the black leather case sitting in his lap, facing the expanse of water out the window.

I toss the comforter off of me and get out of bed, Saint's shirt that I slept in hanging down my thighs as I walk toward him and lean against the back of the chair, resting my chin on his shoulder and looking down at what he's doing.

He startles and tilts his head to look at me, but I'm focused on what he's drawing. It's half of a wolf's face, the other half is a peony. There's so much detail in the wolf with the fine lines of fur, and the peony has a lot of texture in the petals and beautiful shading. It's amazing and I can see why Saint is so highly sought after for his work. He's an artist.

"That's beautiful," I say, still resting my chin on his bare shoulder.

"Thanks," he answers, folding the case closed with the large piece of paper and pencil inside of it. He checks the time on his phone that's sitting on the high arm of the chair.

Walking around in front of him, I push his feet off of the ottoman and sit on it, turning sideways so I can talk to him, but still look at the water without turning my back on him. "Is it for a client?"

"No," Saint breathes, sliding down in the chair and widening his legs around me. "It's just something I've been working on for a few weeks."

I prop an arm on his thigh and lean my head against my hand, watching the sun rise and reflect off of the water. The room brightens with its warm, morning glow. "It makes sense. Your shop and business. With that kind of talent, it's no wonder you're as respected as you are."

I can hear his steady breath behind me. Strong, slow. He's relaxed, content for now. "It wasn't always the plan, but when I quit school and had a lot of time on my hands, I realized that I could turn my hobby into a career. The shop started when my mentor and I got tired of being pushed around by our old shop owner and we went out on our own."

"Where's he at now?" I ask, enjoying the morning with Saint. The rumble in his sleepy, unused voice, the warmth of his body behind me, and the spectacular view of the Sound with the line of mountains on the other side.

Saint chuckles, and I hear his usual self in it. Self-assured, confident, Saint. "He moved. He was losing all of his business to us so he closed up his shop and moved to the Midwest." He leaned forward and kissed my cheek gently, his short beard scratching my face. "Get dressed, my Queen. I'll make breakfast and then take you to your car." I nod when he pulls away, and he stands and starts to leave the room. "You can take any clothing you want," he calls over his shoulder.

Looking out over the water one last time, I see a ripple far out in the water and what I think is an Orca fin.

Pulling open drawers in the dresser, I find a thin, long-sleeved shirt that I can toss over my dress for the bike ride.

I walk down the stairs, the sunlight filtering through the house and bringing a sense of peace over me that I didn't know I needed. This house, it's just so beautiful and calm. I love it here. Saint is standing in the large kitchen, his back to me while he cooks something on the stove. I take a seat at the round table, the same seat as last night, and a few minutes later, Saint sets a clear glass mug and a plate in front of me. A vanilla latte and a western omelet. He sits down next to me with a glass mug of black coffee and the same omelet. I eat and watch him. This feels natural, but I also feel like something is missing. Maybe it's my skincare. I was only able to clean my face with a makeup wipe from an unopened pack I found under Saint's sink last night when I was looking for a toothbrush.

The fresh morning wind coats my face on the back of Saint's bike, the smell of the water and the trees mixing together to make a pleasant, crisp smell. Saint stops next to my car in the hotel parking lot, but when I get off the bike and try to walk away, he pulls me back to him.

"Thank you for last night, Allie," he says over my lips, his lips barely brushing them.

I narrow my eyes on him, watching his beautiful face look up at me. "When are you going to realize I'd do anything for you?"

"Probably never," Saint says before leaning in the rest of the way and kissing me. Long, slow, and perfect. By the time he pulls away, I'm swaying and in a dizzying daze, wanting to get on the back of his bike and hide in his bed all day with him.

Saint finally lets me go and I get in my car and rush home,

still wearing Saint's shirt with my dress underneath and my heels.

When I pull up to my house, I notice a black bike parked in the street out front. Mason sits on my steps, the hood of his hoodie pulled up over his head and hiding his face as he stares down at his phone. I know it's him though, even without seeing his face. First, he's the only one that would still be wearing a hoodie in July. I mean, it's the morning so he can get away with it, but just barely. He'll have to ditch it in an hour or two though. But I know it's him because of the way he so carelessly sits there. The other guys would be more alert. Mason has this silent confidence about him; he doesn't need to boast or puff his chest out to prove that he's a man. He just exists and it's known who he is. That doesn't make any sense, but it's a feeling I can't explain. He just lives his life and doesn't care about what anybody else thinks.

His head picks up when my car door closes, and I watch his eyes scan my body. My unbrushed hair, mostly wiped off makeup, though there's still some stubborn mascara on my lower lash line making it look a little like eyeliner, a large shirt that's clearly not mine, and my stiletto heels.

"Hey, what are you doing here?" I ask, walking up the side-walk to him.

He stands and bends his head, avoiding my eyes and a small smile pulls at his lips. *Maybe he does care what people think, at least me*, I think. "I hadn't seen you in a few days. I brought you coffee and breakfast." His head picks up and he offers me the paper bag and a small cup of coffee.

"Thank you, I stayed at a friend's last night so I'm kind of rushing." I take the items from him, smiling. Mason is like a breath of fresh air that I didn't know I was gasping for. He's refreshing and light. I love the way he makes me feel. Like I'm floating. His eyes slide down to my neck and he cocks his head, his eyes narrow as he stares at me. "Um," I say when he just keeps staring at me.

His eyes snap up to mine again and he smiles. "Right, of course. I wasn't trying to invite myself, I just wanted to drop that off." He gestures to the bag and cup in my hands and takes a step around me and back to his bike.

"Wait," I rush, turning around to face him. He stops, turning around to look at me. "Can we do something tonight? Dinner or, I don't know, pool or something?"

Mason's mouth spreads into a wide smile and it's almost like I can feel his happiness flow between us. It makes me smile too. "Yeah, pool sounds fun. Do you want me to pick you up or meet there?"

I look over at his bike, remembering my arms wrapped around him the other night. "I want you to take me on your bike."

Mason's smile turns into a dirty smirk, and it's the first time I've ever seen that on him. It's a new side to Mason and I like it. "Text me when you're ready for me to come pick you up." He starts to walk backward toward his bike, watching me.

"I don't have your number," I call as he gets further away, a giddy feeling creeping into my bones and making my stomach flutter.

"I'll text you when I get back to the clubhouse."

My eyebrows come together. "How do you have my number?" I yell as he swings his leg over his bike and sits down.

He laughs, shaking his head. "You forget what I'm capable of," he says and starts his bike, cutting off anything I might have said to that. I guess he's got a little bite in him after all.

9

ALLIE

M ASON PULLS US INTO A PARKING LOT WITH A BRIGHT RED FOOD truck and a long line. He holds my hand as I step off of the bike and I watch him lean the bike against the kickstand and turn it off. His long legs swing over and he stands in front of me, smiling down with a big smile, his blue-green eyes sparkling.

Taking my hand, he leads me to the truck and the line. "I know it's probably not your usual choice of food, but this is the best Mexican food in Washington!" he says excitedly, and I look up at him. I love his happiness. He looks ahead of us at the truck, holding my hand tightly as I stay tucked into his side. He's in a navy v-neck shirt and light-wash jeans, with his cut and white Nike shoes. His tan arms are strong and thick with muscle. I'm definitely overdressed for a food truck and pool, but to be honest, I'm usually overdressed for everything. I like dressing up, and I like high-end items. I won't apologize for that. It's how my dad raised me.

"Mason!" the woman taking orders calls from the truck. A few people in line turn around to look behind them and the woman waves us forward with big motions.

Mason chuckles and pulls me behind him as he leaves the

line and goes to a second window, which I think is the pickup window.

"You come here often?" I ask, following behind him.

"A bit," he says before a man comes to the window and leans out, clasping his hand with Mason's and smiling broadly.

"Your usual?" he asks.

Mason looks over the menu that's hanging on the side of the truck, his eyes narrowed. "Yeah, and whatever she wants." Mason pulls me in front of him and rests his hands on my shoulders.

"Uhh." I look over the menu quickly and then place my order.

The man leaves to make our order and the others that are still in the normal line, and Mason steps toward the truck, gripping the window and sticking his head into the truck.

"Hey, mama!" he calls.

"Hi, Mason. Your girlfriend is very pretty!" the woman taking the orders calls back. She leaned back to talk to Mason, but she looked through her window at me before leaning back again.

"I know!" Mason says, turning around and smiling at me.

He leads me to a wrought iron table. Music plays over a speaker somewhere and people sit and eat their food or leave with their orders. The line has only grown since we ordered, and I'm grateful that Mason knew the owners and was able to get us past the line.

When our food is done, Mason goes to get it and brings back the two plates—overfilled with food.

"So you do come here a lot," I laugh between bites.

Mason nods, swallowing the bite of his enchilada. "I do. The guy who took our order is my best friend from high school's older brother, and the woman is his mom." He takes a drink of his water and screws the cap back on. "I come here at least once a week, but usually more. It's nice to get out of the clubhouse sometimes."

"Don't you go to Reese and Callum's?" I take another bite, listening to him.

Mason snorts. "Yes, but this food isn't burnt or over-seasoned." I cover my mouth to hold in my laughter at my best friend. "I love her like she's my little sister, but I don't love her enough to eat that every day."

"You're terrible," I say through laughter. "She's not that bad."

Mason chuckles, and his smile is wide. "She is, but she's getting better with Cale's help."

We eat the rest of our meal in mostly silence, but we both steal glances at each other often, smiling and then laughing every time one of us catches the other looking. Things with Mason are easy and light. I have fun and I'm not worried about how he feels or how I feel. I like him. I like this.

The sun is close to setting, getting lower in the sky and turning the sky a beautiful pink, and the music is still playing from a speaker on the truck. The line has died down, and now only a few people stand in line or wait for food. Mason picks up our empty plates and carries them to a trash can. "Is There Somewhere" by Halsey starts and I softly sing along, swaying on the chair to the music and laughing at Mason's smile as he walks back to me.

He holds out his hand and I take it, letting him pull me to standing. Mason leads me through the tables and stops in the middle, pulling me close to his body and swaying with me, his arms circling around my back and resting above my ass.

"What are you doing?" I giggle, letting him move our bodies back and forth to the song.

"Shhhh." Mason closes his eyes. "Keep singing, I want to hear your voice."

I look around, not able to hide my smile. "Mason, no one else is dancing. Everyone is watching us."

"Let them. You deserve to be seen." He rests his chin on my head and I relax into his chest, continuing to sing along softly.

Cars drive by on the busy road next to us, people sit around talking and eating, and Mason and I sway to the music, lost in each other. I wouldn't change this for the world. I'm right where I want to be. Yet, something small nags at the back of my mind, like I'm forgetting something.

When the song ends, I open my eyes and lean away from Mason, looking up into his beautiful eyes. The sound of people clapping pulls my attention from Mason and we both look around at the few tables still occupied, couples and singles clapping and smiling. An elderly couple sits off to the side and the man is leaning over and kissing the woman while she wipes at her eyes.

Mason twirls me around in front of everyone and a few cheers erupt. I cover my face with my hand and burrow into Mason's side. He chuckles and tugs me along under his arm toward his bike.

"I'm never going in public with you again," I say as he sits down on his bike and pulls the handlebars, bringing the bike upright.

Mason shakes his head and lifts his ass, pulling his phone from his back pocket and checking it. "Cale needs me to install a block on Reese's new phone. You want to play pool at the clubhouse?"

The good mood we were in evaporates with the reminder of Reese's stalker. "But I thought Reese's—"

"He's dead." Mason interrupts.

I shake my head, not understanding. "Then why do you need to install a blocker on her phone again?"

He licks his bottom lip. "Reese's stalker showed us how open all our shit was. Even though the threat is gone, we're still keeping a tight lock on everything." Mason pulls me toward him, and I look down at him on his bike. "I'm only doing this because she got a new phone, not because there's a new threat, okay, beautiful?"

I nod, and he tugs on my hand, indicating for me to get on behind him, but I pause—one more thing holding me back. "Who's going to be at the clubhouse?" Mason's brows tug together, and my brain screams at me to cover for myself, to not tell him about Saint. "Like there's not a party or anything, right?"

Mason's eyebrows soften and he shakes his head. "Nah. It's just Leo, Jack, Nox, and I at the clubhouse. Some girls might be around, but that's usually it on a weekday. The other guys come in here and there, but not so much anymore, they all kind of have reasons to be home now."

I nod once and step onto the back footrest, sliding on behind Mason and wrapping my arms around his stomach, and resting my cheek on his back—the leather of his cut is cool on my face as he pulls out of the parking lot.

10

———

SAINT

Two Weeks Ago...

Of course, it would rain today. Today of all fucking days. It's been clear all week, hell it's been clear and sunny for the last month, but today Mother Nature decides that she's going to weep with us. Rain falls lightly, the sky gray and fog collecting at the tops of the Evergreens.

My black boots have water droplets on the toes, the grass is green under them, and a few feet away, Ronan's casket is being lowered into the ground. I can't watch it. A few cut sluts sniffle on the other side of the grave from me. My brothers spread around me, with me standing in the middle. Reese is tucked under Cale's arm, and Huntley is standing in front of Finn, leaning back against his chest and holding his arms that are wrapped around her. My hands remain in the pockets of my jeans, not really sure what to do with them. I just stare at the grass, rain landing on the blades and sliding to the ground. A woman finishes talking—a cousin Ronan grew up with I guess, I don't know. Killian invited a lot of Ro's family. Killian and Conor stand at the end of the grave, a short Italian woman holding hands with Killian.

People step forward, tossing flowers onto the lowered casket. One by one, my brothers toss a flower and step back.

Digging into my cut pocket, I pull out the small wooden boat I had a local woodworker make for me. It's about the size of my palm and I step forward and drop it onto the pile of peonies. Ronan was Irish Catholic, hence the Wake everyone is heading to after this at the clubhouse, but he and I were always interested in Norse mythology too. Just another thing we shared.

I was the last person to drop something into the grave, and everyone starts for their cars several feet away. My brothers clasp my shoulders on their way.

I keep my gaze focused on the boat, waiting until it's quiet around me, and then I look up at the retreating backs of my brothers. They're all walking together. Callum and Finn are next to each other, their girls on the sides of them. Reese and Callum hold hands, and Mason has a hand on her shoulder as they walk. Allie holds Reese's other hand. I didn't know she was here. Huntley is tucked under Finn's giant arm, with Leo walking next to her and saying something to her, his face turned towards her. Jack walks beside him, his head down. Wyatt, Nate, and Tobi walk behind them, hands in their pockets.

I crouch down, my knees hovering over the open hole. "Fuck you for leaving me. You know they're going to vote me up to Prez." I drag my hand down my face, my eyelids heavy from lack of sleep. "I don't know how to do this without you, Ro. I'm going to find them. I'm going to find who did this to you, and I'm going to bring them here and we're going to end them together. I promise." I stand and walk to the small table that held the flowers, a few left over. Grabbing one, I pull a petal off and drop the petal in the grave, taking the flower with me as I walk to my Audi.

PRESENT...

I don't even know how long I've been sitting here, hunched

over a drawing, redoing the petals over and over again. Frustrated, I toss the pad onto the table, followed by my pencil, and lean back in my chair, looking around the Chapel. I chose to sketch here because I knew that no one would bother me, but some days it's hard to sit here. The painful reminder of him, the want to live up to him, and the worry that I won't. I'm supposed to go to Finn's shop tonight to work on the K-Model. I came here after work because I didn't want to drive all the way home to Orca Bay and then back to Merrill Hill. It's not that far, but I wasn't in the mood. I could hang at the clubhouse for an hour or so and wait.

Pushing my chair back, I gather my stuff, slide it back into my leather case, and head for the door. The clubhouse is quiet, "@ My Worst" by Blackbear plays softly through the open bar area. A single blonde head sits at the bar, talking to Peyton as she leans her elbows on the bar top. I know those bouncy, blonde curls.

Allie.

Her tan back is bare, with two thin, loose straps crossing mid-back, and a pair of tight, black jeans hug her waist.

I walk to her quickly, resting my arm on the bar next to her and glaring at Peyton until she gets the hint and walks away. Allie looks up at me with wide eyes, her mint green eyes shining in the lights. "What are you doing here?" I ask, my head cocked. My gaze slides from her to Reese's purse on the bar next to her. "Oh, you're here with Reese?"

Allie clears her throat. "Um—" she starts, but I pull her hand, interrupting her.

"Come here, I need you for a minute." I lead her back to the Chapel and guide her through the doors, shutting them behind her and pushing her against them.

A groan leaks from her throat and I lean in and run my nose up the column of her neck, her floral scent bleeding into my lungs and anchoring me back to earth. I lick her jaw and then slowly move my lips to the corner of her mouth, gently flicking my tongue against the crease.

Allie moans, and moves her lips, trying to chase mine, but I pull away and chuckle.

"Beg," I demand. Staring into her pleading eyes.

"Saint," Allie whines, and I crash my face to hers, taking advantage of her gasp and thrusting my tongue inside her mouth. My tongue brushes hers the way I wish my fingers were pushing along the inside of her pussy instead. Allie's hands wrap around my neck and she lifts her leg, her knee hooking around my hips and pulling me closer to her. My hands leave her hips and slide up her bare back, one hand gripping the thin straps hanging loosely from her shoulders. For a moment, I think about yanking them and baring her perfect tits to me, but then she'd be left without a top, and I know Allie would have my balls for ruining it.

Pulling away from her, I pull her lip into my mouth and suck on it. "You're mine," I growl, letting go of her lip.

She blinks up at me, her lids heavy and her lips swollen. Smirking, I pull away from her and lean down to grab my leather case that I dropped when I pushed Allie against the door. She steps away from the door, walks over to the mirrored picture, and swipes at the lipstick that's smeared under her bottom lip. I watch her, remembering our first night together on this table. She reaches down and grabs her jeans by the belt loops, adjusting them on her hips and I slip my phone out and take a picture of her, another to add to my collection. I need to leave while she's distracted and there's distance between us.

"I'll see you, my Queen," I say and open one of the Chapel doors, stepping through. Mason is walking down the stairs, our eyes locking and us giving each other a nod. I hear more footsteps coming down the stairs behind him, and the soft feminine tone of Reese's voice. I walk past him and toward the door.

"Hey, have you seen—" he calls behind me.

"I haven't seen anyone," I say, not turning around. I'm sure he's looking for Leo or Jack, he'll find them on his own. They're around somewhere.

MASON

My boot lands deftly on the floor of the clubhouse, my head swinging around, searching for Allie. I left her at the bar when Cale and the Princess came upstairs with me. Heels clicking against the wood floors pull my attention away from the bar, and Allie steps out of the Chapel, her eyes searching around her, and her lipstick mostly gone.

Her soft green eyes meet mine and hers widen, her jaw dropping slightly. I stare at her, and then as the pieces start to slide together in my brain, my eyes swing to Saint's back as he steps out of the door and it closes behind him.

Of course. Of fucking course this would happen to me.

"Thanks again, Mase." Cale slaps my shoulder as he and Reese step around me.

I keep my eyes on Allie. "Yeah, of course, brother." Fuck, a brother. Allie is sleeping with a brother. And not just any brother, but my fucking President.

"Are you coming over for dinner this weekend?" Reese asks softly, placing a hand on my arm.

I tear my eyes away from Allie, looking down at Reese. "I'll be there, Princess." I smile at her. Fuck me. Why Allie? Anyone but her.

"You too, Allie." Reese grins at Allie, whose eyes are still slightly frantic.

Allie nods quickly and Cale finally pulls Reese away, stopping at the bar for her purse, and then leaving the clubhouse.

I wait until they're gone before saying anything. The silence stretches between us and becomes thick.

"Saint," I sigh. "You're with Saint." I scrub my hand down my face.

"No!" Allie rushes out, hurrying toward me. "We aren't." She pauses, looking at our feet and shaking her head. "We aren't together, we've slept together a few times, but he won't take it any further." Her head rises and she looks into my eyes.

I take her chin in my hand, loving how soft her skin is. "You deserve to be more than someone's secret fuck."

She shakes her head, her eyebrows drawing in. "It's not like that either. He's not ready. Not while he's dealing with Ronan's... Death." I flinch at the word.

I mull that over in my head, and Allie watches me. Her eyes bounce between mine. Saint is a fucking idiot, but his mistake is my gain, and I don't plan to make the same one he is. "So he hasn't claimed you?" Allie shakes her head, the corner of her bottom lip pulling under her top teeth. "Okay," I say.

"Okay? Okay, what?" she asks.

"Okay, we can keep seeing each other without me getting my cut and balls taken from me." I let go of her chin and run my hand down her bare arm, wanting to keep touching her.

"But what if I want to keep seeing you both?" she asks slowly, looking up at me from under her lashes.

"I," I pause. That can't happen. Two brothers in the same club? There's no way that will work. We will kill each other—or more so—Saint will kill me or kick my ass out of the club. I just got my cut. I shouldn't risk this, I shouldn't go against my President. Brothers share—women included—but Allie isn't a club whore. Things would be different with her. I look into her eyes, her pleading, mint green eyes, and I crumble. "I'd do anything you ask, just please mourn me when he kills me."

Allie chuckles and buries her cheek into my chest, her arms wrapping around my stomach and holding onto me tight.

I suck in a breath, the faint lemon scent of her hair filling my nose and I look down at her soft blonde hair. I wrap my arms around her shoulders and listen to her breathing. This is exactly where I belong, where I want to be for the rest of my life. I know it now.

SAINT

The door to the clubhouse slams behind me and I drag my hand down my face, feeling a little remnant of Allie's lipstick on my lips. Looking up, I notice a man standing next to my bike. I have no idea who he is, and although there's a bike in the lot that doesn't belong to any of us, he isn't a biker; he's not wearing a cut. And this bike is not a Harley, it's a Ducati Penigale. He's staring at my bike, not realizing I'm coming up on him.

"Can I help you?" I snap, eyeing the guy.

He slowly turns to face me. "Sorry." He smiles. "I'm assuming you're Saint?"

"And you are?" I cross my arms, slipping one hand inside of my cut to where my gun sits inside of my cut pocket. I didn't always carry a piece anymore, but when my President was gunned down and we still don't have any leads, I started thinking maybe it'd be a good idea to start up again.

"Ace." He runs a hand through his white hair, his brown eyes trailing down my body, and pausing on my hand slipped inside of my cut. His eyes meet mine again and he raises an eyebrow. "I was friends with Ronan. He wanted me to give this to you if anything ever happened to him." Pulling my hands free of my cut, my brows pull together. What does he mean? Ace pulls a manilla envelope out of his leather jacket and hands it out to me, and I stare at it.

"Why weren't you at his funeral if you were friends with him?" I ask, looking him up and down. Expensive jeans, clean shoes, expensive leather jacket.

Ace scoffs, and his lip pulls up at the edge. "I saw what you all planned. You know he wouldn't have wanted something like that." I feel like someone punched me in the gut. I do know he wouldn't have wanted something like that.

"I didn't plan it, his cousin did," I say softly.

"His cousin didn't know shit about him. You and I both know Ronan didn't participate in his religion anymore." I nod, my eyes drifting to the ground. Fuck, he's right. Ronan would have hated that graveside funeral, the only part he would have actually enjoyed was... "I was at the wake though for a little bit, now that, Ro would have enjoyed." I snap my eyes up at him again. "Oh yeah, I was there. You spent the majority of the night in your Chapel. But here, take this." He pushes the envelope a little further toward me.

Taking it, I turn it over and see my name written in Ronan's neat handwriting. Ace walks away silently, leaving me with whatever the hell this is.

"Who are you?" I look up and yell after him.

He reaches his bike and turns around, pulling a helmet on. "I told you. I'm Ace."

"What do you do? How do you know Ronan? How the fuck did you get into my clubhouse?" Why the fuck are my gates open when it takes a code to get into our compound?

Ace smirks and slides his dark sunglasses on. "I do a little of everything, Ronan and I went way back, and maybe take another look at your security. There are some weak spots."

"What the fuck?" I whisper as Ace mounts his bike and speeds off, his engine roaring as he goes.

I put my drawing case in my saddlebag and sit on my bike, tearing open the envelope gently.

My hands shake as I pull out a single piece of paper, Ronan's writing covering the front and back. Taking a deep breath, I open the letter and start reading.

Saint,

I'm sorry, brother.

I'm sorry I left with so much unfinished shit between us and with the club, but I know you can pick up where I left off and continue on. You can make the dreams we had for the club come true. The expansions, the renovations, the new money ventures, all of that shit is possible with you. You just have to believe in yourself.

The club is your home, Saint. The guys are your brothers. Lean on them now that I'm gone and use them to keep you level. The club needs to come first now, you're their President. I chose you as my VP because I knew one day I wanted you running the club. I knew you could do it, and you have to do it now.

Now that you've met Ace, he can help you. He was always my last resort, my saving grace, my calvary. He will be yours too, but he really does need to be your last resort. If you ever find yourself backed into a wall and you have to fight for your life, Ace will save you. No questions asked. But his favors come with a heavy price tag, and you only get one for free. The prepaid with this letter has Ace's number in it. It's his emergency line, and he knows you have it now. I hope you never have to use it.

Lead the club to new heights and never look back. Don't trust anyone but your brothers. Open up more and show them the man that I know. More than just Cale and Finn deserve to know who their President is. Guide and teach the new guys. Teach them everything that I taught you: how to thrive in this world, and how great it feels to be free and on the back of a bike.

This is your club now, you need to lead it how you want, but I hope that you'll take some of my advice.

You're doing a good job, Saint, just like I knew you would.

I love you, brother, just like you were my own.

-Ronan

CLEARING MY THROAT, I look into the folder, and sitting at the bottom is a prepaid phone, just like Ronan said. I fold the letter and place it back into the envelope and into the saddlebag with my drawing case. Today has already been enough of a day without the letter, and now there's some mystery man? I slide on my dark sunglasses and pull out my phone.

SAINT:

I need you to look into someone. His name is Ace. Oh yeah, and come fix our fucking gate.

MASON:

Ace? Got a last name? What happened to our
gate?

SAINT:

No, but he was just in our lot, so work your
fucking magic and find him. I want to know
everything there is about him. He said he knew
Ro. Whoever he is, he got past our gate, so fix it
and make sure it doesn't happen again.

MASON:

Got it, brother.

I pull up to Finn's shop, parking right outside of the bay with
the large garage door open, and turn off my bike. Finn steps out
of his office, finishing off a water bottle and tossing it into the
recycling bin as I walk into the shop. There are a few cars parked
in the other two stalls, but everyone seems to be gone, but us.
"Habits" by Machine Gun Kelly is playing over the big speakers,
but it's turned down so it plays softly in the background.

Walking by the classic bike, I pat the handlebars and keep
going to the chair that's sitting at the back of the shop. Finn sits
down on a short rolling stool—the poor thing looking like it
should give out under his big body—and rolls over to the side of
the bike, turning to look at me.

"Okay, so I thought we could start by going over the vision
you had for the bike," Finn says.

Nodding, I lean back in the stool and grab the beer bottle
that someone left for me on the workbench behind me. "Right.
So what Ronan and I were planning was..."

ALLIE

"CAN WE GO UPSTAIRS AND TALK?" I ASK, PULLING AWAY FROM Mason's chest and leaning my head back to look up at him.

He stares down at me, his arms sliding down to loop tightly around my back. He nods and lets go, taking my hand and leading me up the stairs.

The hallway is narrow, with old white walls and the same warm wood flooring from the first level. White doors line the hall on both sides, all of them closed. He stops about midway in the hall and pulls his keys from his pocket, sliding one into the lock and unlocking the door. Inside is a king-size bed with a plain, navy comforter and pillows, a small wood nightstand, a tall dresser next to the door, and a long desk with two monitors set up, with a black gaming chair in front of it. Mason holds the door for me and I step inside and look around while I walk to the bed. Mason closes the door behind him and walks to his desk, turning around the chair and sitting in it, across from the bed.

Our knees brush as I sit on the bed in front of him, my back straight, while he is hunched over, resting his elbows on his knees and watching me.

"How are you okay with me wanting to see both you and Saint?" I ask, sucking my lips between my teeth.

Mason releases a slow breath. "Do you like me?"

My shoulders deflate and I reach out to rest my hands on his knees, next to his elbows. "So much more than I thought I ever would."

"I like you too, a lot. And I don't want to give up on us when Saint hasn't made any claims on you. He's never mentioned you and never showed any interest in you." I flinch at his words and he scrunches his nose. "Sorry," he says. "But he hasn't claimed you, so you're fair game, which means he can't do anything about you and I getting to know each other."

I nod, taking in what he's said. That makes sense. Even when Callum and Reese weren't together, people at least knew she was his. No one knows there is anything going on with Saint and me. Our faces are inches apart and Mason's breath fans over my lips when he speaks. "And I don't suppose you'd want me to claim you, even though I gladly would."

I shake my head and watch hurt flash in his eyes before it quickly disappears and Mason pastes on a small smile. "Not yet," I answer, hoping it doesn't sound like a rejection, because it's not.

Mason nods gently. "Then you figure it out with Saint, and we'll figure it out with us." Mason sits up, pulling away from me. "God, I just hope you don't dump me for the grumpy asshole." We both laugh at the same time and I follow Mason, sitting up on the bed. "Are we good now?" Mason asks, resting his arms on the armrests of his chair.

"Yeah." I nod. "We're good."

"Great! How about I take you home and I take the long way, maybe make a few detours to make it even longer?" Mason stands and pushes his chair back to his desk.

"Sounds perfect." I take his outstretched hand and let him lead me out of his room.

———

MASON'S BIKE pulls to a stop in front of my house. My porch light glints off of a single head of red hair sitting on my porch steps, Callum's Raptor sitting in my driveway.

"I should probably tell her about us," I say, leaning forward and speaking into Mason's ear.

"Yeah, you probably should," he answers, a smile in his voice.

Stepping off of the bike, Mason helps balance me. "Thank you for tonight, I had a lot of fun." I stay standing next to his bike.

Mason grabs my hips and pulls me into him. "So did I. Will you be at Leo's housewarming party?"

I shake my head. "Reese hasn't said anything about it."

"Well, I'm inviting you. We can go together or I can give you the address."

Smiling, I nod. "Yeah, okay. When?"

Mason's lips slip into his beautiful smile, teeth showing and light beaming from him. "This weekend. Let me know if you want me to pick you up."

"Okay." I nod, not able to wipe the smile off of my face.

"Great," Mason whispers as he pulls me into him and reaches up to guide my face to his.

He kisses me slowly, taking his time to slide his tongue with mine, slowly learning me and figuring out how our lips can work together. It's a perfect mesh of lips and tongues and by the time he pulls away, I'm in a daze. My head is cloudy and my heart is thumping wildly in my chest. Mason makes me giddy and excited, he makes me feel like I'm in high school with my first boyfriend, getting my first kiss. I love this feeling.

I back away, watching him for a few steps before I finally turn around and face my best friend sitting on my steps, smiling like a child.

"Why are you sitting outside? You know the code to the house." I ask when I reach the porch, Mason waiting by the curb, his bike rumbling, and Callum sitting in his Raptor with the engine off. His window is rolled down, and he's watching Reese and me.

"It was a nice night, I wanted to enjoy it," she says, leaning back on her elbows and staring up at me.

Shaking my head I sit down beside her and my eyes fall on Mason again. He waves when he sees me sit and pulls away from the curb, driving down the road, the roar of his bike getting quieter the farther he goes.

"So you and Mason?" Reese squeals. "I love that!" She bounces on the step next to me and I laugh quietly. This must be a dream come true for her. Two of her best friends getting together.

"Yeah, it's nice. He's nice." I lean forward and rest my elbows on my knees, laying my chin in my hands.

"I don't know who to warn, you or him." She laughs.

I look back at her over my shoulder. "What do you mean?"

Reese looks at me like I'm dense, her head cocked and looking at me out of the top of her vision. "You've never been in love, Al. Every boyfriend you've ever had has fallen head over heels in love with you, and you've left them when it became too much." She leans forward and wraps an arm around my shoulder, probably because my mouth is hanging open in disbelief that she said that. "I just don't want you to hurt him, Al. Mason's a great guy. But I also know that he hasn't had anything serious in a long time, and I don't want him to hurt you either."

Sighing, I shake my head. "I've never felt this way about anyone, Reese."

Reese smiles, her green eyes lighting up and it makes me want to hug her so tight she can't breathe. She's my best friend, has been since Freshman year of college, and I'm so happy that she found Callum, even if it did mean she had to have a killer stalker to find him. "I think you two will be good for each other. Just be honest with him, okay?"

Pulling away from her, I turn so I can face her on the steps. "Actually, I already have been, and I kind of need to talk to you too?"

Reese straightens, blinking a few times. "What do you mean?"

"I'm kind of seeing Mason *and* Saint," I say slowly, picking at one of my nails.

"Saint?" Reese gasps, her eyes wide. "I had no idea..." she trails off, looking to the side. "But I should have, you two were always tiptoeing around each other and sneaking off together!" I give a small smile. It's not that we're actively trying to hide anything, but we're also not announcing whatever it is we're doing. "Wait." She holds up her hand and shakes her head. "You're dating both of them... at the same time?" Her brows pull together and her eyes narrow.

"Well, not really." The picking gets a little more frantic as I try to sort out my thoughts. "Mason and I are seeing what we are and where we could go, but I care about Saint. A lot." I glance up at Reese and see her watching me, but I don't see any anger or judgment in her eyes so I continue. "I'm helping him get through his grief from Ronan." I watch Reese's shoulder deflate slightly and she bites the inside of her lip.

"So you're going to continue to see them both? Do they know?" She scoots closer to me and I lean into her, needing her support in a physical form right now.

"Yeah, I am. I need to see it through with both of them." I let out a long breath. "Mason knows, but I haven't figured out how I'm going to tell Saint yet."

Reese purses her lips and looks at the ground. I know she's going to say something I won't like, that's her tell. "This isn't going to work, Allie. Bikers are extremely territorial, especially over their women."

Looking out over the lawn and road in front of us, I shake my head. "I care about both of them. I can't choose between them."

I turn to look at Reese and she nods, leaning into me and wrapping her arm around me again, hugging me from the side while we stare at the stars and enjoy the warm night.

14

MASON

CODE SCROLLS ACROSS THE SCREEN—LINE AFTER LINE—AND I press my fingers into my eyes, clearing away the blurry vision. I've been staring at this screen for close to eleven hours and my eyes are starting to cross.

"So you got anything for me?" Saint's voice startles me.

I jerk in my chair, turning to face him walking into my room. I didn't even hear him open the door. "Jesus, Saint. I've had three too many energy drinks today, you could have given me a heart attack!"

Saint stares at me, a bored expression on his face—or maybe that's just his face. Either way, he's waiting for me to answer. I gesture to my bed for him to have a seat, and I spin around to face him.

"I couldn't find anything. Literally anything. No Ace that matches his description, nothing on his registration for his bike, and nothing in relation to Ronan. I didn't even get a hit when I ran him through facial recognition. It's like he's a ghost."

Saint sighs, his jaw flexing. "I'm tired of not having any damn answers." You and me both, brother. I had to make sure that I scrubbed through Ro's phone well enough, so I reached out to

Miles to crack into Ro's phone. He didn't find anything, so I'm safe, and I can tell Saint that I'm doing everything I can to find Ronan's killer, even though I'm not. "How'd he get into the compound?"

I spin around and click out of my program, pulling up our feeds. "That, I do have some answers to." I hear Saint's shoes hit the floor behind me and I know he's looking over my shoulder at my computer. Pulling up the feed from the other day, we watch the video play. A man rolls up to the gate, light hair, a black leather jacket, and a nice street bike. He holds his phone up to the box where we have to enter a code, and after a few seconds, he pulls it away and types in the code, messes with his phone again and then the gate slides open. He drives through and then waits by Saint's bike for him until he leaves the clubhouse.

"What the fuck just happened?" Saint asks.

I rewind the video so I can explain as it happens. "He used some sort of app to override our system. It gave him the code to the gate and then sent him the confirmation instead of us. He accepted and the gates opened for him. It didn't alert us because the system thought it was one of us."

Saint glares at the screen like he can force the answers out of the video with his ire. Shit, if anyone could it'd be him. "Tell me about the app, is that a common thing?"

I pull up the screen with the code again and shake my head. "No. Someone had to make it for him, or he made it himself. Now that I know how he got in, I looked through the system and found his code. It's an older way to code, so either he's an old schooler or the program is older."

"That's it?" Saint asks, not rudely, just pushing to see if there's more information.

"Hackers usually leave some sort of calling card in their codes, so I'm working through that now to try to find who made the program. That should either point us to him or whoever made it for him. They've hidden it well though, so it's taking a little longer, but I'll have it soon," I say absently, scrolling through the code again.

"Okay, let me know when you find something." I nod and Saint walks to my door. "You fixed the system right?"

I pull another drink from the drink fridge under my desk. "Yeah, now it will alert me when there's any movement at the gate, that should alert us before someone can even access the box."

"Send that to me too," Saint says, stepping through my door to the hallway.

I turn back to my screens. "Got it, Prez!" I call after him as he leaves.

One more scan-through while I finish this drink and then I'll take a nap. This is the fun part of hacking and coding. Finding people and what they're hiding. This is what I do, this is what I'm good at.

15

ALLIE

"So, you're going with Reese and Cale to Leo's housewarming party that *I* invited you to, and we can't hang out there together?" Mason's voice echoes through my phone as I pull my champagne-colored, one-shoulder, loose dress off of the hanger and walk over to my shoe shelf. The dress hits me about mid-thigh and hangs loosely over my body.

Grabbing my nude, YSL platform sandals, I answer, "It's not exactly like that." Squeezing the phone between my ear and my shoulder, I carry my clothes from my small walk-in closet to my bed and lay them down. "Saint will be there, and I haven't told him about us, and he deserves to hear it from me and not have it shoved in his face without warning."

Mason sighs. "You're right, but he should hear it from both of us. Sneaking around could be exciting, but this is the only night we do it. I'm not hiding you, Allie."

Grabbing the phone with my hand—and relaxing my shoulder—I grip the top of my robe and smile to myself. I like this side of Mason—slightly possessive, and wanting everyone to know we're together. "Deal. Maybe we can sneak away and find a private part of Leo's cabin."

"Oh, we're definitely doing that." Mason's voice turns husky and I squeeze my thighs together in response.

Hanging up, I take my hair out of the towel and start getting ready.

———

CALLUM PARKS his Raptor in front of a modest cabin deep in the woods. Light shines out of the windows and people mingle about everywhere. Some stand outside on the grass, holding drinks and talking, while others are standing on the low porch. I walk beside Reese, with Callum on her other side, holding her hand. Bikes and cars are parked everywhere, and I can hear the thumps of bass bleeding from the house before we even step inside. "Swim" by Chase Atlantic becomes clearer when we step into the cabin. An open space—the living room and kitchen are all one space—with the front wall all windows that look out onto the front porch and the yard. Leo is sitting in a leather armchair, a blonde woman hanging over the back of the chair with her arms wrapped around his neck and whispering in his ear. Finn sits opposite Leo in a matching leather chair with Huntley perched in his lap, rolling her eyes at Leo. But directly in front of us are Jack and Mason, sitting on the long couch. Jack leans forward and talks to Finn while Mason stares at me, a small smile pulling at his lips. Reese leads us in and pushes me onto the couch next to Mason while Callum sits on the other side of me and Reese lowers herself onto his lap.

Mason's cologne seeps into my senses, his smell taking over and making me relax. He drops his hand and rests it next to mine, hooking his pinky into mine and holding it while he watches Finn and Jack talk, nodding every once in a while and humming in agreement.

I look around the cabin, half interested, half looking for

Saint, but I don't see him anywhere. The interior of the cabin is all wood; the walls, the ceiling, the floor, the cabinets, and the countertop in the kitchen. Leo broke it up with leather furniture and a cream shag rug under the couch and chairs. Leo leans forward, a dollar bill rolled up, and inhales two thin white lines off of the coffee table in front of us. Blinking at his bent form, I take in the scene. I didn't even notice anything on the table when I walked around it to sit down.

Finn looks away from Jack and snaps at Leo. "You better not let that shit get out of hand." Finn leans forward, pointing at the white powder laying on the table.

Leo leans back, resting his head on the back of the chair, the woman that was behind him earlier steps around the chair and kneels in front of him, taking the bill and turning around to lower her nose to the remaining lines. "Calm down, daddy Finn, it's a party."

Finn leans back in his chair and returns his attention to Jack, but Huntley releases an angry breath and stands, walking to the kitchen behind us. She walks by Leo and smacks him on the side of his head as she strides past. Mason snorts next to me, Callum barks a laugh, Reese's mouth hangs open as her shoulders shake with a silent laugh, and Finn smirks, his eyes following Huntley to the kitchen. Leo holds up his middle finger to Huntley, but she doesn't pay him any attention.

"Bikers," I say under my breath, shaking my head.

"I thought you liked bikers," Mason whispers, bringing his beer bottle to his lips. I can see a small smile on the corner of his lips as he stares forward.

I open my mouth to say something back, but I stop when the front door opens and Saint steps through, the new Prospect, Nox, following in behind him.

His face is set, but when his eyes land on me, they stay on me as he walks in and passes us to walk back to the kitchen. He claps Leo on the shoulder as he passes us.

Fidgeting in my seat, I look over my shoulder and see Saint leaning over the counter and grabbing a bottle, then he turns around and leans against the counter and we lock eyes. I turn back around and slump into the couch, out of the corner of my eyes, I can see both Mason and Reese watching me.

This is so uncomfortable. I shouldn't have come.

Pulling my pinky from Mason's, I wring my hands in my lap and stare at them. I can feel Saint's eyes on the back of my head and I don't know what to do. I'm sitting next to my kind of boyfriend, and I can't do anything with him, but I also can't go to my other kind of boyfriend, because no one knows about us. This is so complicated, but I can't find it in myself to regret anything.

"Go talk to him," Mason whispers in my ear as he leans into my side, putting his arm over the back of the couch and tapping Reese's arm that's draped behind Cale on the back of the couch.

Reese looks down at us and smiles, nodding. Going with Mason's ruse, I guess. I chance a look at him and see a sad smile on his face and it breaks my heart. I don't want him to be sad or hurt. Guilt hits me hard in the chest and I stare at my hands again.

"Go, it's okay," he whispers again, removing his arm and taking his peaceful presence with him.

I swallow the lump in my throat and stand, walking around the couch and toward the kitchen where Saint is still leaning against the counter. I have to tell him. Now. I don't ever want to see that hurt in Mason's eyes again. I won't. I just hope I don't hurt Saint by trying to save Mason.

I step up beside Saint, my hip hitting the counter and I look up at him.

He cocks his head slightly and looks down at me from the

side of his vision. Tears prick my eyes at the emotions that overcome me when I'm next to him. The awareness that I would already do anything for this man. That I'm so far in over my head and he has no idea.

"You look thirsty," a voice says from the other side of the kitchen peninsula.

I jerk my head toward the voice and see Nox holding a beer bottle out to me. I release a breathy laugh, taking the bottle from him. "Thanks." Turning back to Saint, I say, "Can we talk." I pause. "About us?" I lean into Saint's side, whispering.

Saint lifts the bottle of vodka to his mouth, taking a long drink. "There is no us, Allie."

I jerk away from him, narrowing my eyes. "How can you say that?"

He stays looking forward like I'm not even here. "Because I told you there couldn't be. Not right now."

I stare at the short sleeve of his white shirt, my vision blurring with tears. Setting my bottle gently on the counter next to me, I leave without another word.

With every step to the door, I feel my heart clenching and my stomach rolling. Someone opens the large glass door as I get to it, and I turn sideways to squeeze past them as I step outside onto the porch.

I walk aimlessly, Saint's words replaying in my head over and over. His bored tone and the lack of emotion in his eyes as he stared forward. The thin heel of my platforms sinks into the ground, but I keep walking. It's dark, the lights of the house behind me, and I step onto a small wooden dock. I didn't realize Leo had a pond in front of his cabin. You couldn't see it when we arrived because of the darkness, but up close, I see it.

I wrap my arms around myself and watch the still water, the moon reflecting off of it and providing little light.

Warm arms wrap around me, and I can tell it's Mason before

he speaks. His fresh scent is similar to the soft scent of the trees we're surrounded by. "What happened?" Mason turns me to face him, and I press my face into his chest, inhaling his scent. "Are you crying?" Mason lifts my chin so my face angles to his.

"There's nothing there. He said there wasn't anything there." I shake my head. Saint's face taking over my vision instead of Mason's dark shirt.

"He'll realize it," Mason soothes, his thumb stroking my cheek.

I lick my lips and reach up, pulling him down to my lips.

A car drives up to the cabin, its headlights shining on us.

"What the fuck?" a venomous voice snaps.

All heat leaves my body as I pull away from Mason, staring at the headlights shining on us and squinting. Saint steps in front of the lights, his face twisted in a snarl.

Saint stalks toward us and Mason steps in front of me, holding his hands up in a placating gesture. Saint's eyes widen a moment before he lunges at Mason, pulling him away from me by his throat and turning and throwing him to the ground, following him down.

"Saint!" I scream, hurrying toward where Saint is straddling Mason, throwing punches to Mason's face and sides while Mason tries to shield himself. I run around them, almost twisting an ankle as my heel digs deep into the soft grass. I drop to my knees at Mason's head and lean down, trying to get Saint's attention as I yell his name again, this time right in his face. He doesn't stop.

Loud footsteps pound the ground behind me, and a large body pulls Saint off of Mason. Finn's arms are wrapped around a still-swinging Saint, and Callum steps in front of them, grabbing Saint's hands. I look down at Mason and someone else drops down next to me. Reese's musky perfume wafts over me and I look up into her concerned eyes.

I focus again on Mason. He's staring up at me, and tears fill my eyes. What have I gotten him into? What have I gotten myself into? He moves to sit up, and I pull him closer to me so I can look at his injuries. One eye is starting to swell and blood is pouring from his nose, which looks broken. My hands tremble on the sides of his face. I want to touch him, but I don't want to hurt him, not more than I already have by dragging him into this.

Mason reaches up with one hand and pushes my hand onto his cheek. "It's okay," he says. "It could have been a lot worse."

I shake my head, tears falling down my cheeks. "It shouldn't have happened at all!"

"Don't fucking touch her!" Saint bellows from the dock. Finn still holds onto him tightly and Callum steps in front of him to block his view of us.

Everyone is staring at us. People left the house to watch us from the porch.

Letting go of Mason, I stand and walk to Saint and the two Outlaws restraining him.

"I was going to tell you," I say slowly, my hands reaching out to him, but stopping short.

Saint's eyes widen and he looks from me to Mason, then back again. He looks me up and down, a disgusted sneer lifting his top lip. He jerks away from Finn, and this time the tattooed new VP lets him go. "You were going to tell me that you're a club whore now?" Saint's words leave his mouth in a biting tone, and I feel them flay me. Finn and Callum walk away and just Saint and I stand on the dock.

"I'm not..." I trail off, shaking my head.

Saint takes one step toward me and is in my face, his eyes burning and our chests touching. "You can't ride on the back of my bike and then lay under another man. If you want to be a club whore then fine, but I don't let whores bounce on my dick."

"I care about him, Saint. I care about both of you." My voice wavers, the tears streaming down my face. I've never seen Saint like this. He doesn't show a lot of emotions... ever.

"It's either me or him, Allison." Saint stands rigid, looking down at me.

My mouth opens and I look down at his chest, considering. Finally, I shake my head lightly. "I can't choose between you."

He leans forward slightly, speaking into my ear, but not whispering. "Then I'll make the decision for you." He straightens and his shoulder shoves against me, pushing me back.

I watch him stalk up the slight incline of the lawn. People are scattered around watching us, but far enough away that they probably didn't hear anything. Except for Callum, Finn, Reese, Huntley, and Mason. Finn and Callum stand closer than the rest, ready to intervene again if needed, and Reese and Huntley stand next to Mason, who holds his side but watches us intently. Saint doesn't look at anyone as he passes, just stares straight ahead until he gets on his bike in the driveway and speeds away, the motor roaring as he leaves me behind.

I watch his bike for as long as I can, which isn't long, and when it's out of sight, my eyes drop to the ground, and on autopilot, my feet carry me away from the dock. When I get next to Reese, Huntley, and Mason, Reese reaches out for me and drags me under her arm. I look up at Mason. His sweet eyes, holding concern when they should be holding anger or resentment. "I'm so sorry," I whisper.

He reaches out with one hand and cradles my cheek, his thumb swiping at the tears that are still falling.

"Don't be. This didn't change anything for me." He looks at Reese. "Get her home, okay?" Reese nods and Mason leans in and places a gentle kiss on my forehead.

"Come on, Jack will take you to get your nose fixed in Leo's wannabe race car." Finn places his hand on Mason's shoulder and leads him away. Jack and Leo are standing between us and the crowd at the front of the house.

Reese pulls me along with her to the cars with Callum following behind us.

"I guess no dinner tomorrow, huh?" Reese whispers.

I chuckle, wiping my eyes. "Let's reschedule."

16

SAINT

I didn't know where I was going until I got here. I just drove, my hands white-knuckling the handlebars, going way over the speed limit, passing people when I probably shouldn't have, and then I came to a slow stop here.

The marble headstone is cold against my back as I slide down it and sit in the grass.

"I almost killed him, Ro," I whisper, leaning my head against the stone. "If he wasn't a brother I would have. I would have slit his throat and left him at her feet while he bled out. All over a fucking girl. A girl that led me on and pretended to be there for me while she was fucking another brother under my nose."

A loud rumble carries on the wind and I know that I've been found. Someone came to check on me. Of course they did. They're supposed to be there for me, even when I feel like pushing everyone away and shutting in on myself.

A black bike stops next to my newly painted white one, and a large body walks toward me. It's gotta be Finn, his wide shoulders giving him away.

Sure enough, Finn's face becomes clearer in the dark when he gets closer, and when he reaches me he crouches in front of me, resting his hand on the top of the headstone and hanging his head.

After a moment, he lifts his head and pulls his hand away, falling onto his ass in front of me. "I figured I'd find you here."

"Why'd you come?" I look at Finn from the bottom of my vision.

He shrugs, not letting my surly mood affect him. "I'm your VP, I should be the one you confide in." He bends his long legs and wraps his arms around them. "You're my brother and I love you. We all know you're hurting, and I thought maybe you'd finally talk to me."

A rough laugh escapes my throat. "What is there to talk about? I can't do anything to fix any of this."

"You can tell me about Allie." His dark blue eyes watch mine and I bite the inside of my lip. Why the fuck not, maybe it would feel better to confide in someone. This grief and now losing Allie feels like a fucking hurricane inside of me and I don't know how much longer I can shoulder this storm. Every day it feels like I'm drowning, and I just lost my only solace. Though I guess I never actually had her, did I?

"She said she'd wait for me, and then tonight I found her kissing Mason. She just told me what I wanted to hear, and then she fell into his bed too." I don't even know what the fuck happened. She had seemed so sincere. Why did I not figure out she was a lying bitch?

"Why was she having to wait for you?" Finn asks, his head cocked.

I bring my head forward, staring at my legs. "I can't give her what she deserves right now, not when I feel like I'm dying most days. She doesn't deserve to save me, I need to do it myself. And right now all I can focus on is finding out what happened to Ronan, and she deserves someone's full attention." Shaking my head, I let out a bitter laugh. "I guess she realized that and found someone to give it to her."

"She's the one who should decide what she deserves," Finn says gently, watching me.

"You don't think I know that?" I snap. "A woman like Allie is someone who you give your everything to because she's a woman that will only come into your life once, and I couldn't let myself fuck it up by not being there for her." I lick my lips, taking in deep breaths to calm down. "I thought she was okay with what we were doing, as much as I hated making her wait, I thought she was okay. She never said anything about..." I trail off, swallowing hard. "I hate her." I mean it. I don't feel anything for her besides hatred and resentment.

Finn nods silently and stands, offering me his hand. "Come on, let's go start an afterparty at the clubhouse. Get you drunk, or fucked, or high. Whatever will get you out of your head for a while." Clubhouse, oh fuck.

"How's Mason?" I ask, pulling on Finn's hand and standing.

"He's okay. Leo took him to get checked out, but I think he just has a broken nose."

I stare at the ground. It's not often that brothers throw hands. "I kind of feel bad," I admit.

Finn shrugs one big shoulder. "It could have been handled better, by all of you."

Nodding, I turn around and place my hand on top of the speckled gray headstone, running my hand over the rough top of it. I drop to a crouch and kiss my index and middle finger, pressing it into the emblem of the Outlaws that's etched into the stone above Ro's name.

17

ALLIE

THUNK. I PULL THE DOOR CLOSED, TURN MY KEY IN THE LOCK, AND turn around. I stall in my steps as I see Mason walking up my driveway toward me. Running down the steps, I collide with him, wrapping my arms around his stomach and holding onto him tightly.

"I was just on my way to the clubhouse to come see you," I say into his soft tee shirt.

Mason strokes my back with one hand, the other tangled in my hair and holding my head to him. "I'm not staying at the clubhouse right now." Mason presses a soft kiss to the top of my head and I pull away, leaning my head back to look up at him. He has two black eyes, one much worse than the other, and his nose is bandaged. It doesn't take away from how handsome he is. His ocean-green eyes stand out brighter against the dark bruising and his jaw seems sharper than usual in the early morning light.

"Because of Saint?" I ask. I hate that he took the fight for me. That he laid there and didn't fight back. That Saint attacked him. God, thinking of Saint makes my stomach hurt. My heart clenches so hard I think it's going to explode. I hurt him too. He walked away from me last night and I know that was the last time. He's done.

Mason shakes his head. "No, I just wanted to get away. Give us both some room to breathe."

Reaching up, I brush Mason's brown hair out of his eyes, my fingers tracing his temple. He closes his eyes and leans into my touch, his tongue barely reaching out and wetting his lips. "Stay with me," I offer.

His eyes open wide. "Really?"

Nodding, I burrow into him again. I love the feel of his strong arms wrapped around me. Holding me close to him, even after everything that happened last night. "Yeah, Sophie's been spending a lot of time at Logan's. It'd be nice to have you here."

I can feel Mason's smile when he presses a kiss to my forehead. "Okay, I'll go get my stuff from Miles' and come back tonight."

"Okay." I nod against his chest and hold him tighter.

Mason's finger slides under my chin and lifts it to look into his eyes. "Get to work before you're late. I'll see you tonight." He leans down and glides his lips along mine, I chase his mouth and he finally gives it to me, pressing soft kisses to my lips before he pulls away and walks backward to his bike, smirking and leaving me in a daze.

I'll be really early for work if I leave now, but I guess I can stop and get breakfast.

18

MASON

THE ROOM SPINS PAST ME. COMPUTER SCREENS, BLACK WALLS, AND neon lights all blur together as I spin my chair in another circle. I lean my head against the back so I can watch the white ceiling spin instead.

"You are the most annoying person I have ever met," Miles drawls, boredom laced in his tone. I don't blame him. He was in here before I went to see Allie this morning, and now it's afternoon. I'm not sure what he's been working on. He sat me on the other side of his desk when I told him I needed to look through some code. He was so kind as to lend me a monitor so I could hook it to my laptop and run it that way. It's a lot slower. My laptop just doesn't have the power that my desktop back at the clubhouse does, but this will work for what I'm doing.

"You know, the guys told me you lived like you were in a cave. I pictured you holed up in some underground shelter. Not this." I think about his forest house that has glass for most of its exterior walls. It's like he's living outside. He's really secluded though, and his security is crazy. Two gates to enter the property and cameras everywhere. He seems paranoid, but I guess when you hack things for a living, you probably rack up some enemies.

I stop spinning so I can look at Miles. He's already looking at me from between two of his monitors. His face is the epitome of boredom, but I know it's just him. He's perpetually grumpy, and my constant excitement just makes him retreat more. I still consider him a close friend though, and I know he feels the same about me. He wouldn't have let me crash here if he didn't. "Am I a hermit?"

I think that over. "A little. When's the last time you left the house?"

Miles narrows his eyes. "Last night. Before you crash landed on my doorstep with a broken nose."

As I'm about to reply, my computer flashes that its search is done. I abandon the conversation for my results. Pulling them up, I scan through where the trace led me.

No. Fucking. Shit.

"What?" Miles asks. Oh, I guess I said that out loud on accident.

I shake my head and look over my results again, there's no way. But no, I'm right. "What do you know about Shadow?"

The clicks of Miles' keyboard stop abruptly, and silence fills the room. "Are you referring to—"

"The world-famous hacker who single-handedly shut down the nuclear threat a few years ago by hacking in and disabling their codes? The one who exposed that Garrett Wycoff was getting the money for his presidential campaign from a ring of child traffickers? The most accomplished hacker in the world? Yes, yes I'm referring to *that* Shadow."

"Uhh." Miles draws out the word. "Well, I guess that. Why, what did you find?"

I stare at the screen in disbelief, and a lot of worry. "The person who created that app that hacked our security system was Shadow."

Miles pushes his chair back so fast it rolls into the wall behind him, but he doesn't spare it a glance as he storms around the desk and leans in behind me, scanning my screen. "No shit. I've never seen their work personally. They never fuck with small shit, like scanning apps."

"I know." I shake my head. "It's a few years old, but still, Shadow's signature was buried deep in the code. I almost missed it... again." I've gone through this code four times and was about to give up on the fifth when I finally find it.

Miles stands back up and walks back to his chair, pulling it away from the wall and back to his desk. "I'd be worried about the guy that walked into the compound, if he has connections as high as Shadow, you don't know what he's capable of."

"Maybe if I could find out who Shadow is, I could find out who Ace is," I muse aloud. After some time of silence, I look up and realize Miles is watching me. "What?" I ask. He's biting his lip and staring at me. It dawns on me, and my eyes widen, no doubt looking like they're about to pop out of my head. "You know who Shadow is?"

"No." Miles shakes his head, his floppy brown hair falling into his face. "But I know someone who might be able to contact them."

"Who?" I rush, almost yelling at him. "We have to ask them to connect us!"

Miles sighs and rubs at his eyes with his fingers, taking a short pause. "For Ronan," he says before he starts typing furiously.

Rushing around his desk, I stand behind him and watch him pull up a sketch looking chat room. It's obvious it is on the dark web. Chats scroll by with creepy as fuck messages and I realize it's some sort of online bulletin board where anyone can post anything. Miles types in a series of numbers and then waits. I stand behind him for a while, both of us watching the messages roll in, in silence. After a while, I walk back around the desk to pull my chair up next to him.

Miles and I watch the screen, leaving for bathroom breaks, and he sends me to the first gate to pick up the food we ordered. We make small talk, all while Miles watches the messages. Finally, about five hours later, a series of numbers pop up in the chat, and Miles quickly copies and pastes them into the bar at the top. It takes us to another chat room, but this one is private.

> I need to get a message to Shadow. Can you do that?

Miles types.

> What is it?

The person sends back immediately.

> I need to know who Ace is. He says he knew a friend of mine that died. Ronan McKenna, Former President of the Devil's Outlaws.

Miles sends.

> You know what it will cost you,

They say... Or post.

> I'm aware.

Miles types back

> They'll be in contact if they agree.

They send and then the chat closes.

"That's it?" I ask, staring at the blank screen.

"That's it," Miles answers. "Hopefully Shadow will reach out to us, but there's no guarantee.

"What will it cost you?" I ask cautiously.

Miles scowls at the screen. "My Japanese Gold Star Espeon and Umbreon pokemon card set."

I bark a laugh and then suck my lips between my teeth when Miles' head snaps to me and he glares at me. "I'm sorry," I say, trying to hold in my laugh and failing.

"They went for twenty-two thousand at auction two years ago!" he yells.

"For pokemon cards?" I ask, my eyes wide. What the fuck? I was always a baseball card kid myself.

"They're rare!" Miles shakes his head and takes a deep breath.

"I'm sorry," I say again. Kind of meaning it this time. Damn.

Miles sighs and pushes back from his desk. "It's fine." He stands and stretches his arms over his body. Miles is tall as hell. He's Finn's height, but a lot thinner. He'd be lanky if he didn't have muscle—not a lot, he's kind of lean. "He'll need a favor one day and I'll get them back." Miles heads for the door. "I'm going to take a nap. I'll let you know if Shadow contacts me.

I thank Miles as he leaves the office and close down my laptop, taking it to my room and changing so I can hit Miles' gym.

IT'S BEEN a few hours since Miles wandered up to the third floor and I came down to the first to use his gym. I texted Allie when I first came down and told her I probably wouldn't be coming over tonight—that I was working—but she said it didn't matter how late, just come by when I was done. Which was such a relief, because I really wanted to see her. I need to get this shit figured out though, I've been stalled for weeks with no clue of where to go next, and I finally have something to follow. I'm in the middle of stirring a stir fry on the stove, staring out at the trees surrounding Miles' house, when I hear bare feet slapping on the concrete floors. Shaking my head to get my drying hair out of my eyes, I turn around to look at him and watch him walk from the stairs over to the large island behind me. He's shirtless, with sweats on, and his eyes still half closed.

He moves his tattooed hand down his face. "Smells good."

"It's almost done. You want some?" I turn around and stir it again.

Miles grunts and I hear the barstool skid across the floor. "Bowls are in the cabinet next to you."

I pull out two bowls and pile the food into them, pulling at a few drawers before I find the silverware. I take everything over to Miles and sit down next to him, handing him one bowl with a fork in it.

We eat in silence. Miles gets up a few moments later and fills two glasses with water, and brings them back to us.

We've gotten comfortable with each other in the months that he's spent helping me with the hacking stuff. I learned a lot of stuff in school, but Miles taught me how to use it in a different way and to think of things differently when creating codes. He taught me to think like a criminal. I've gotten to know his surly personality, and how quiet he is. He's similar to Saint, and I think he's come to tolerate my endless talking and optimism. He's a cool guy, and he's smart as hell.

Miles' phone vibrates on the concrete island and he glances down at it with his full fork halfway to his mouth. The fork clatters in the ceramic bowl and Miles hurriedly picks up the phone, swiping it unlocked and bringing it to his face.

I slowly set my fork down too and lean my arm on the counter, watching him. "Is it Shadow?"

Miles nods. "Well, I guess we got an answer." Miles passes me his phone and I snatch it from his hand.

A picture from an unknown number. I click on it and release the breath I didn't realize I was holding. It's a picture of Ronan and Ace. Ronan's arm is slung around Ace's shoulder. Ronan's pitch black hair and Ace's bright white, complete opposites. They're laughing, and with the wear on the picture—even with it being a scanned photo—and the lack of faint laugh lines around Ronan's eyes, I can tell the picture is from several years ago. I'm guessing ten. I stare at the photo. My eyes focused solely on Ronan. I miss him so much. I only knew him for almost a year, but he was still a brother. It's not fair what happened to him.

I finally hand the phone back to Miles. "That's it?" I ask.

He stares at the phone, locking it after a moment and placing it back on the counter. "That's it."

Shadow didn't give us Ace's identity, but they did confirm that Ronan knew Ace and they were great friends. I didn't realize how many secrets Ronan was keeping from the club, and it makes me think of the others. Saint was hiding Allie, and Jack is one thousand percent hiding something, but I'm not sure about Leo. Finn and Cale are all loved up and living their best lives, they don't have anything to hide anymore. It makes me a little upset; I thought we were closer than that. I didn't think there would be secrets between brothers.

But I'm a hypocrite, because I'm hiding the biggest secret of all. They would all hate me if they found out what I did.

That thought leads me back to Saint. Fuck, I have to show this picture to him. Update him on what I found. My ribs still ache, and they will for a while since one is cracked. I'm not saying I deserved what I got, but I wasn't innocent. I knew Allie was his girl, and I moved in, telling myself it was fine because he hadn't claimed her. We were both wrong, which is why I didn't fight back.

I don't think he'll take my call, so I pull up a message to him instead.

MASON:

I found something about our visitor.

Saint takes a while to reply, which I kind of anticipated.

SAINT:

Meet me at the clubhouse. I need to talk to you.

Aw fuck, he's totally going to take my cut.

19

SAINT

THE LAST THING I WANT TO BE DOING RIGHT NOW IS WALKING INTO the clubhouse to talk to Mason. But he said he had information on Ace, and I need to apologize for what happened at Leo's cabin. Even though my stomach still rolls at the thought of Mason and Allie, I need to make it right—he's a brother.

He can have her.

Mason is already waiting at the bar for me when I step into the clubhouse. Peyton smiles at me and refills Mason's glass. Looks like water. He looks over to the door and turns to face me when he sees it's me walking in.

"Chapel." I point and walk past him.

I hear his footsteps follow behind me, his boots hitting the wood floor in time with mine.

Pushing open one of the chapel doors, I flick on the light and make my way to the head of the table. I pull out the large chair and sit, staring at the table for a moment. This still doesn't feel right. I shouldn't be here. Mason takes his usual seat, which is three from my right, on the other side of Cale's seat. He doesn't have to sit there—this isn't an official meeting—but I'm glad he did. He's out of reach in case I fly into a fit of rage again. Fuck, I must have broken his nose. His eyes are black and his nose is a little swollen. I actually feel a little bad.

"Alright, what did you find out?" I ask, resting my forearms on the table.

Mason shifts, pulling his phone from his back pocket and then settling back in the chair. He talks as he messes with his phone. "I was going through the code from the app and was able to find someone's signature."

"Who?" I interrupt.

Mason looks up briefly and then back to his phone. "It was created by one of the best hackers in the world. No one knows who they are, they just pop in and save the day by hacking shit and then disappear back into the shadows," he chuckles. "Actually, they go by Shadow."

"So Ace is Shadow?" That would make sense. That's how he got in, how he knew everything about all of us.

Mason shakes his head, his brows furrowing. "I don't know." I purse my lips, resisting asking what the fuck he does know, and he continues. "Miles was able to get in contact with Shadow, and they sent us this." Mason slides his phone across the table to me, and I lean forward and grab it. I pick it up and all of the air leaves my lungs.

Ronan is standing with his arm slung around Ace's shoulder, and they both have huge grins on their faces. The picture is several years old—Ronan looks young. Ace looks young. There's no doubt that Ronan knew Ace. The letter was undoubtedly from Ronan. They were friends. I'm not worried about whether Ace is Shadow. It doesn't matter. Actually, it would be better for us if he was and we ended up needing his help.

This was a nice distraction, and it feels great to have some answers after so long, but this doesn't answer what we've really been looking for. What the fuck happened to Ro?

I slide Mason's phone back to him, staring at the table and

trying to burn the picture of a smiling Ronan into my brain. "Okay, thank you." Mason grabs his phone and slides his chair back. "Wait," I say, snapping my head up as he starts to stand. "I just wanted to make sure we were good after I uh…"

"Fucked up my face?" Mason laughs.

I roll my eyes. "It's not that bad."

Mason shakes his head, his chuckle tumbling out again. "We're good, Prez. I don't think I would have done anything differently if I had—"

"We don't need to talk about it," I interrupt. "We can leave it at 'we're good.'"

He nods once, his smile thin. "Got it, brother."

"Alright," I say as a dismissal and lean back in my chair. Mason takes the hint and stands wordlessly, making his way out of the Chapel, through the door we left open.

When I'm alone, I try to replace my thoughts of Allie and me on this table, and then Allie and Mason on the dock, with the smiling picture of Ronan.

I take a deep breath, let it out, and stand. Pushing in my chair, I tap the top of it twice before leaving the Chapel and shutting the door.

I'm going to do whatever it takes to find out who killed him and make them pay. I don't know when it'll happen, and I don't know what else I'll lose in the process, but I'll make it happen. Nothing else matters anymore. Not sassy law school students with thick thighs and a big ass. Not blonde, bouncy curls hanging over my cut while she wore nothing else and rode my cock. Nothing.

20

ALLIE

My toes sink into the lush carpet as I walk down the hallway of my home. Since Mason said he was going to be a while, I decided to take a bath and spend extra time on my skincare. I'm carrying an insulated cup of water back to my room, my silk pajama shorts and tank top swishing against my body as I walk.

I hear the creak of a floorboard behind me and pause, looking over my shoulder. I only see the dark hallway. I continue to my room. Sophie is staying at Logan's tonight, as she does most nights now, and I'm home alone, like most nights.

Setting my cup on my vanity, I sit down and start to brush my hair out, then reach into a drawer and grab my hair oil. I hear another creak and I look into the mirror on my vanity to see behind me.

A man lunges at me as soon as our eyes lock, and I scream. My entire body lights up in fear. My focus sharpens and I feel like time stands still and speeds up all at once. The man in black lays one gloved hand on my shoulder and pulls my torso back into him as his other hand slaps a cloth over my mouth. I hold my breath, refusing to breathe in the fumes I'm sure are on the cloth, and grab the closest thing to me—my hair oil.

This will have to do.

I fling it over my head, aiming for him, and after a few shakes of the bottle, the man hisses and staggers away, dropping the cloth and rubbing his eyes. I suck in a giant lungful of clean air. I know my time is limited—I don't know how hair oil affects the eyes—but I'm sure it won't put him out for long. I have to find something else to defend myself with.

Grabbing my insulated cup from my vanity, I charge him, standing slightly bent over in the middle of my room, and hit him over the head with the stainless steel cup.

Once.

Twice.

He staggers, his hands leaving his eyes and going to his head. I hit him again. And again. His knees buckle underneath him and I hit him again, causing his body to fall face-first on the floor. I collapse to my knees and hit him again for good measure, and then I sit there and watch to see if his back moves with breaths, to see if he's going to lunge at me again. I watch and I don't look away. I don't even think I blink.

Until I heard my front door open and close, and slow footsteps descend down my hallway. Heavy footsteps. Not Sophie. Tears fill my eyes, and I know that I'm very low on options. My fingers shake around the bloody cup that I'm holding, and when the man walking down my hallway enters my room, the cup slips through my fingers, hitting the carpet with a soft thud.

I look into Mason's soft gaze and relief rushes through my body, almost to the point of being overwhelmed, and I let the tears fall.

Mason rushes to my side, angling my face to his and running his thumbs over my cheeks. "What happened?" he whispers, his eyes darting to the man and then back to me.

"I don't know. I heard something and looked up and he was there. He put that cloth over my mouth and nose, but I—" I blink rapidly.

"You did good," Mason soothes, pulling me into his chest. "But I'm going to take care of this for you, okay?" He separates us with his hands on my shoulders and looks into my eyes. "Take off your clothes and go sit on your bed."

My brows pull together. Get naked? Right now? "What?" I ask softly.

Mason's hands smooth down my arms. "Your pajamas are wet and bloody. I'm going to get rid of them."

I quickly look down at my top and shorts, and he's right. I guess my cup wasn't closed. The majority of the water is on my carpet, and I think the man. At least, I hope all of that wetness is water, but some did get on me, as well as spots of blood splattering my chest and the top of my tank top.

I stand and step away from Mason and the man, stripping while Mason holds his fingers to the man's neck. I crawl onto my bed and sit in nothing but my panties. Wringing my hands and watching Mason press his fingers to the man's neck, I ask, "Is he alive? Did I kill him?"

Mason pulls away and pulls a scary-looking knife from a holster at the back of his jeans. "Not yet, but he's close."

Mason presses the blade to the man's neck, but before he can go any further I shout, "Wait!"

He turns around, eyes widened. "What?"

"You can't just kill him! In my house!" I demand.

Mason drags his tongue along his lower lip, and I'm too out of it right now to even appreciate it. "Why not?"

I sputter. Noises leave my mouth while I try to form my thoughts into a sentence. "I'm in law school, Mason! I can't be an accomplice to murder!"

Mason stands and strides toward me, and my eyes take in his

form, his scowl, and his demeanor. This isn't my Mason. This is the Outlaw Mason. The one who can kill and get away with it. The one who runs the state and doesn't take shit from anybody.

"This man does not get to walk out of this house tonight. The only way he is leaving is in a bodybag, and I don't care where you go to school, who your employer is, who your dad is, or what you plan on doing for a living after school. None of that is changing my mind." He leans down and runs his lips over mine, staying close as he says, "So please, either close your eyes or watch, but I promise to take care of this. No one will find out what happened here tonight." Then he pulls away and I take in a deep breath to center myself, drowning myself in Mason's comforting scent.

He walks back to the man, kneels down, and stabs him in the base of his skull. More blood spills on to my already-soaked carpet, and I watch the cream color turn an ugly shade of red.

I think about the man. Who he might have been. Did he have a family? A wife? Kids? He had to have a mother. A father. But then I remember that he was in my house without permission, and he was going to do something to me. Kidnap me, rape me, kill me. I don't know, but I don't think anything good could have come from him chloroforming me from behind while I struggled. I decide that I won't feel bad for protecting myself and that I won't feel bad that Mason killed him to protect me.

Mason killed him to protect me. I repeat that in my mind several times. Killed him. For me. A wave rushes over me. So many emotions, it's hard to separate them all, but I can pick out one clearly.

Love.

I'm not sure if Mason loves me, and I'm not sure I'm in love with him, but right now, I know that I feel love toward him. The only other person who ever protected me was... Saint. My heart aches at the thought of him and fresh tears well in my eyes.

But then someone pounds on my front door.

"Merrill Hill Police!" My eyes snap to Mason's at the same time his snap to mine. He's still kneeling next to the dead guy, sliding his phone back into his pocket.

He stands and rushes toward me. The knees of his jeans are soaked in blood. Oh, God. We're going to prison. "Get in the shower. Wash your body, wash your hair, and do not get out until I come get you."

I blink, trying to gather my thoughts. What the fuck do I do? I'm trying to run through cases in my head, things I've learned in school, but everything is blank right now. "I can help us. He attacked me, it was self-defense!"

"Now, Allie!" Mason whisper-yells. "Do exactly as I say." His eyes bore into mine and I listen. I stand and hurry for my door, casting one last glance over my shoulder because I'm not sure if I'll see Mason again after this. He's already tossed his cut on my bed and is pulling his shirt over his head. I turn around and run for the bathroom, closing myself in and rushing for the shower, doing exactly as Mason said.

21

MASON

Fuck, fuck, fuck. I pull my shirt over my head and hurry out of my jeans, adding them to the pile of Allie's clothes. Grabbing my gun out of my cut, I run into the kitchen in just my boxers and wash my hands, getting the blood off of them. Why did I choose to kill him in the messiest way? I was so angry—so scared for Allie—that I let it cloud my judgment. At least I didn't shoot him though, the cops might have heard that and rushed in instead of knocking.

Once my hands are clean, I turn and rush to the door as a hand pounds on the door again. Setting the gun on the entry table behind the door, I swing the door open and stand in front of the police. Two cops look over my exposed body, then look at each other before focusing back on me.

"Can I help you, officers?" I ask politely, breathing heavily from my jog into the kitchen and then to the door.

"We got a call about a woman screaming." One of the male officers tries to look around me. I check his name badge: Officer Kay

Smirking, I rub my hand over my jaw. "Uh yeah, that was my

girlfriend." The officers watch me intently. "I can assure you, she is just fine."

"Can we speak to your girlfriend, sir?" Officer Kay asks, looking around me again.

I flip on the light that's next to the door, the living room lights up and I see the cops looking down at my Outlaw tattoo on my pec.

"She's in the shower washing off, her legs were pretty wobbly on her way there, but sure, I can go get her." I step away from the door.

"Can we wait for her inside?" he asks. The other cop walks toward the steps of the porch and looks around the neighborhood, maybe at the neighbor who called, I don't know.

I shake my head, smiling. "Do you have a warrant?" I pause for an answer, even though I already know the answer to it. "I don't think Allison Lenkov would appreciate me letting cops into her house without a warrant."

The cop that was looking around comes back. "That won't be necessary. Thank you for talking to us, and sorry for interrupting your night, sir." He tries to pull his partner away, but Officer Kay doesn't budge, looking at him with confusion. He yanks him away and whispers in his ear, but I catch what he says. "He's an Outlaw and Allison Lenkov is the daughter of Alexei Lenkov. We don't want to be on either of their radars."

He's right. The Outlaws own most of the police force, though not all, obviously, and Alexei Lenkov is a powerful lawyer in New York City with major ties to the Russian mafia—or rumored to, at least.

The man laying dead in Allie's bedroom probably has to do with her father. Maybe a guy he jammed up, or someone trying to attack the mafia through him. Maybe he's just a creep who knew two girls lived here. I'm not sure yet, but I intend to find out. The cops wave goodbye and leave the porch, sliding into their car and driving away. I shut the door and hurry to the bedroom, grabbing my phone and going to the bathroom.

I should be glad that Allie's neighbors would call the police for her, but they really could have fucked us over tonight.

Knocking softly on the door, I push it open and walk into the steamy room. "All's clear."

The water shuts off and I hear the shower door open. "What?" Allie calls.

Opening the door further, I poke my head in. Allie is standing in the shower wrapping a towel around her, steam billowing out around her. Her hair is wet and slicked back off of her face, and water droplets glide down her body and into the towel. She's beautiful. Free of makeup and the tight clothes she wears; the heels, and the expensive bags. She's breathtaking in all of her forms, but this one is my favorite.

I clear my throat and focus on her mint-green eyes instead of her bare legs. "They're gone. We're good."

Allie nods, her eyes trailing over my body. "You should shower."

I look down at my hands. I only did a quick clean on them. "Yeah, I probably should." I look back up and watch Allie drop the towel on the ground and step back into the shower stall. Her body is exposed and every curve I've dreamt about at night is bare for my eyes to explore. She's even better in person.

My throat swallows roughly and I can feel my cock strain against my boxers. "I don't want to be out there with him." She turns the water back on and watches me, leaving the door to the shower open.

I take that as my invitation and step out of my boxers, walking to the shower to join her. "I already called someone to come pick him up. Get rid of him. No one will ever find him."

I close the door behind me and step under the hot water, lowering my head and letting the water soak it. "I need to know everything. I won't be able to sleep until I know we're in the clear."

Water drips off of my face, and I lift it and turn to face her. "I called a doctor that will take his body, sell whatever he can of him on the red market, and then get rid of whatever else he can't. I don't know the specifics, but I'm pretty confident that he sells the rest to a cult in Tennessee that practices cannibalism."

"Oh my God." Allie's mouth drops and her eyes widen.

"I'll call Leo and Jack after the Doctor leaves, and they'll come over and we'll rip up the carpet and we'll burn it at the compound or Leo's cabin. Someone will need to come in and redo your floors. Maybe you can hire Cale, have him come over on the weekends and pay him?" Allie stares at me while I speak, blinking, but not saying anything else. "It'll make sense for him to fix your floors since he's engaged to your best friend." I turn around to look for something to wash my hair or body, something to look at besides Allie's naked body. "No one will know about this besides us, Leo, Jack, and the Doctor." I see Allie's hands reach around me and grab a bottle and a hot pink loofah. I can feel her round breasts press against my back, her hard nipples teasing me, and I take in a deep breath, trying to calm myself.

The loofah softly lands on my back and I jolt forward, surprised by the touch. Allie washes my back in silence and then turns me around with her hands on my hips.

She runs the loofah over my abs, her eyes watching her hand as I watch her face. "Thank you. For taking care of everything."

"I'd do anything for you," I mindlessly answer, but it's true. Nothing has ever been more true.

She looks up at my words, and we stare at each other. Paused in the moment. I feel something shift between us. Something slots into place and I realize that I've been yearning for this woman for months, and now that I finally have the chance to have her, I will not let anything or any*one* get in my way. Allie will be mine. For the rest of my life. I know it.

Allie washes my chest, my arms, and hands, and when it's time for me to wash my hair, she steps out, leaving me to think over what happened tonight. I can't always be here to watch her, to keep her safe. I recall the bloody cup and the almost beaten-in skull of the man who attacked her—though maybe she doesn't need me as much as I think.

I rinse my hair and turn off the water, pushing the door open to find Allie standing on the other side, wrapped in a new towel and holding one out to me. "Thank you." I take the towel from her and quickly run it over my hair before moving to dry my body. "I think you should come stay with me at the clubhouse."

"What?" Allie gasps.

I raise my eyes from my drying to look at her. "Only until I find out who this guy was and why he was in your house." Allie worries her bottom lip. "Look, I know it's not what you're used to, but it'll keep you safe." That's the understatement of the century. I've seen the pictures of her dad's townhome in New York. Her moving to Merrill Hill and moving into a modest, two-bedroom new build was her slumming it in comparison. I can't think of anything else though, nothing else that I would allow. Allie still doesn't look convinced, so I try harder. "Please, just a day or two, until I know who he was."

Finally, Allie nods and I breathe a sigh of relief.

At the sound of a knock on the front door, I lean down and kiss the top of Allie's head. "That's the Doctor. Wait here, I'll bring you a change of clothes." She doesn't say anything as I leave the bathroom for the front door.

22

ALLIE

I vaguely feel Mason's arms unwrap from around me and his body slowly slide away. My eyes slowly open to Mason's small room at the clubhouse not that I could forget that I agreed to stay here. I woke up at every small sound; the wind outside, Jack or Nox coming and leaving, when Mason snuck away to his computer. I roll over and watch Mason walk to his bathroom and shut the door. He convinced me to call in from work, so I don't have anything to do today except go pick out new flooring with Callum and annoy Mason. I can't go home, not until Mason figures out who that guy was, and I don't want to go to my friends' houses because I don't want to put them in anyone's line of sight.

The door opens and Mason steps out of the bathroom with a towel wrapped around his slim waist, walking to his dresser that's next to it. He pulls out clothes and gets dressed, and I lay in his hard bed watching his firm ass as he bends and pulls on boxers and jeans. The tight muscles of his back flex as he pulls on his shirt. I miss my bed. It helped a lot to have him with me last night, though. Anytime I was spooked by a sound or remembered seeing that guy in my mirror behind me, he was there.

Holding me tightly and making me feel safe. It felt great, but in the back of my mind, I was missing Saint. Not wishing I was with him instead of Mason, but wishing that he was here too.

"Where are you going?" I ask when Mason moves to his desk and pulls his cut off of his chair.

"Church. Downstairs. You can stay in bed, I'll only be gone for a little while." Mason walks to where I'm laying in bed and leans down, placing a kiss on my forehead.

"What are you guys meeting about?" I ask when he pulls away. His eyes dance around the room and he sucks his lips between his teeth. It sets in exactly what they're going to be discussing. "It's about me, isn't it? You told them?"

"I killed someone last night, Allie. I had to tell them," Mason says calmly.

I toss the comforter off of me and shoot to my feet, stalking to my overnight bag on Mason's dresser and pulling out a cream, oversized, chunky knit sweater, a pair of distressed denim shorts, and a simple pair of black YSL sandals. My hair air-dried last night after my shower and it falls in slight waves over my shoulders.

"Allie, you can't—" Mason starts.

"I'm coming, Mason. This is about me, I deserve to be there." I pin him with a look that lets him know I'm going whether he likes it or not.

He sighs and walks out of the room and I follow closely behind him, finger-combing my hair as we walk down the hallway.

When we get to the bottom of the stairs, I see all of the guys walking into the room that I guess is the Chapel. Where Saint and I had sex for the first time. Where I found him drinking alone and looking like the most miserable person I'd ever seen. Leo is one of the last guys to go in, right in front of us.

He eyes me over Mason's shoulder. "Uhhh." He points to me.

"I know." I hear Mason say in front of me.

We step into the room, Mason stepping aside so he can close the doors behind me and my eyes collide with Saint's at the end of the table. My heart locks up and my breathing stops. I didn't even think about seeing him, but of course, he would be here. His eyes narrow and I feel tears threaten to spill, but I hold them off. Now is not the time.

Mason pushes me forward with his hand on my lower back. He stops at a chair and pulls it out for me.

"Absolutely not. Get the fuck out of my Chapel, Allison!" Saint snaps, pointing to the door as I take a seat in the chair that Mason offers me.

I turn to him, pinning him with a hard stare that I hope will stand to the hateful glare that he's casting my way. God, I really hate when he uses my full name. "If you're going to be talking about me, I want to be here, Saint."

"We don't always get what we want, Allison, but I guess that's not something spoiled brats are used to." Saint leans forward over the table and continues to glare at me.

My eyes widen, taken aback by his words, but before I can say anything back, Finn cuts in. "It wouldn't be a bad idea for her to be here. She can fill in any questions we might have."

Saint turns his poisonous glare at Finn and the two stare at each other for a tense moment.

Finally, Saint leans back and looks out over the table, ending on me. "Your wish, my Queen." I feel a pang in my heart at his name for me. He used to say it with adoration and warmth, but now it feels like an insult. He said it with such disgust this time. "It's your floor, Mason," Saint says, leaning back in his chair.

Mason rests his arms on the back of my chair, and I can feel his breath ghost over my head when he takes a deep breath. "Last night someone broke into Allie's house." I move my eyes to my hands in my lap, but I feel eyes watching me. "I called the Doctor for him."

"Who?" Saint asks, and I chance a look up at him and he's staring at me with hard eyes.

"I'm still getting information on him, but it looks like he's connected with the Russian mafia," Mason says, and I whip around to look at him. He bites the corner of his lip and stares down at me.

"The Russian mafia?" I ask, my voice wavering. What the fuck does the Russian mafia have to do with me? Why are they coming after me?

"You don't know anything about your dad and the Russians in New York?" Saint asks, slight amusement lacing his tone.

My head snaps back around to Saint. "No!" I almost scream. Panic seeps into my bones and sets me on edge. "What do you mean my dad and the Russians?"

Saint smirks and looks away from me, and back to Mason. "Figure out what—"

"What do you mean?" I interrupt Saint.

Saint glares at me again. "This is my Chapel, Allison, and I'm allowing you in. Don't interrupt me again," Saint growls. I blink and push into the back of my chair. Seeing him be the President of an outlaw club is kind of scary, especially when he's not my biggest fan right now. His eyes go back to Mason's and he continues. "Figure out what her dad has got going on with the Bratva, and look into who the guy was. Is everything taken care of from last night?"

"Yes. The Doctor took the body. I'm running scans for him right now, Jack and Leo ripped out the carpet last night, Nox is sitting surveillance on the house, and Cale is going to replace the flooring this weekend." Mason lists off everything he set up last night.

Saint nods and picks up a wooden gavel like he's a damn

judge. "Alright. I know you guys have to get to work. Get the fuck out." He bangs the gavel onto the table and chairs scrape against the wooden floor as everyone hurries out of the room. Saint, Leo, Mason, and I are the last ones in the room. Leo and Mason lead the way out of the room, and I can feel Saint walking behind me, his glare burning holes in the back of my head.

Mason walks through the open door, and as I'm about to follow him, Saint's arm shoots out and slams the door closed in front of me. He pushes me against the door, and I look down to watch his long fingers flick the lock.

Saint moves away slightly and I turn around, his chest is almost brushing against mine and I can smell his intoxicating scent.

Fists pound on the door and I turn my head toward the sound, but Saint pulls my chin so I'm looking up at him. Demanding my attention.

"Are you okay?" he asks, his features hard to read.

I lick my bottom lip before answering. "Yeah." I nod.

"You can't stay at home until we figure out who this guy is. You can take a spare room here." Saint lets go of my chin and reaches for the lock behind me.

"Mason said I could stay with him." Saint lets out an angry breath and his jaw clenches, but he stares at the door. I don't want this to be over yet. I don't want to feel the crushing chill that will set in when his body leaves mine. "Can we talk?" I rush out.

Saint pauses, his hand still reaching behind me, but he looks down at me from the side of his vision. "About what?"

I bravely place my shaking hand on his arm, and he looks down at the contact. "About us. About what happened."

Saint swallows roughly and looks into my eyes. Something other than rage finally breaking through his ice-blue eyes. "Forget him," he pleads.

The banging continues, but I feel like something just crushed me. I should have known it was always going to end in a one or the other situation, but it doesn't make it hurt any less. I don't know how I came to care about two men just as strongly, but I did, and I don't want to be without either of them. "I would do anything for you, Saint. Kill, steal, lie, or cheat. Leave everything I've ever known to fall into your world head first, but I cannot do that. Please let me love you both."

"Love?" he asks, his brows pulling together.

"I could." I nod gently.

Saint looks away and I know that I lost him. "I would rather gouge my own eyes out than watch you love someone else, especially a brother," he spits the words out.

I tighten my grip on his arm. "I need you. I need you both," I beg.

He yanks his arm from my grip, glaring at me once again. "I guess that's just too fucking bad."

Saint unlocks the door and jerks it open, stomping out into the hall.

"Saint!" Mason yells after him, his fists clenched at his sides. He was the one banging on the door, but I already knew that.

"She's fucking fine, Mason. Fuck off!" Saint shouts without turning around. He bangs his way out of the clubhouse. Mason, Leo, and I watch him go.

23

MASON

Allie stares after Saint as he stalks out of the clubhouse, slamming the door closed behind him. Her lower lip trembles, but she holds her chin high. Seeing her like this makes me regret not fighting back when Saint laid into me at Leo's party. At the time, I thought he needed to release some aggression, and I was more than willing to take that from him. I did go behind his back. But now I wish I had at least knocked him once for the shit he says to Allie.

I toss my arm over Allie's shoulder, startling her out of her daze. She looks up at me from under my arm, a watery smile appearing on her face.

"Come on, let's go upstairs. I think I have something that will cheer you up," I say, directing her to the stairs.

"Oh!" Leo coos from beside us. "Can I watch?" He smirks.

Rolling my eyes, I move past him. "Not like that, perv." Allie chuckles but lets me step in front of her and pull her up the stairs with me. I can hear an extra set of footsteps on the stairs, so I know Leo followed us anyway. "If you're going to follow, you could at least bring up an extra chair," I call behind me, and footsteps pound down the stairs.

We all step into my room, which Allie and I left open. I walk to my desk and pull out my comfortable chair, offering it to Allie.

I log into my computer and close out the windows from last night. Leo rushes into the room and I take the chair from him, setting it in front of my computer—next to Allie—and continuing hacking into the account.

"What are you doing?" Allie asks, watching the screen I'm running the program on.

Smirking, I gain access to the account and pull up the recurring orders. "Getting a little bit of revenge for you."

Leo lands on my bed behind us, the sound of his body hitting the mattress evident in the quiet room. "Well, I can tell nothing fun happened in here last night."

"Leo, shut the fuck up," I sigh, continuing with my plan. He's exhausting. Does he ever stop thinking about sex?

"I fail to see how you ordering pink gloves is going to get revenge for me," Allie speaks, ignoring Leo.

"Well this is Saint's account, and he has a standing order for black latex gloves for his shop," I say, confirming the order change and smiling at the computer.

"And you're changing the color to hot pink," Allie continues. She chuckles menacingly. "He's going to lose it."

"You two are so boring," Leo yawns, standing and leaving the room.

Turning to Allie, I see her small, content smile pulling at her lips. "That was nice, thank you."

Licking my lips, I smirk as another idea comes to mind. "We can send him confetti dicks too. The package will explode when he opens it, and he'll be cleaning up little plastic dick confetti for months!"

Allie covers her mouth with her dainty hand, hiding her laughter behind it. "We can do that?" The beautiful sparkle reemerges in her mint-green eyes and I feel a peace settle over my heart. She's back. My girl is coming back.

"Beautiful, I could have a human heart sent to his front door. Of course, dick confetti can be done." I shake my head, pulling up the website.

Allie is quiet beside me, so I look over at her. Her eyes are wide and her lips are pressed together tightly. "Let's not do that."

"Whatever you want, Blondie." I wink and pull up the completely legal website for the dick confetti.

Allie watches me order it, and then walks over to the bed, laying down on her stomach across it, and orders food to be delivered to us. While she's doing that, I pick up where I left off on my search for the guy who broke into her house last night. I had the Doctor take his prints and send them to me before he played fucked up mortician on him. I've been running them through databases in New York and haven't gotten anything, so now I'm trying federal and international databases. This guy was definitely a professional. Hopefully, at some point, he fucked up and got caught up with the law.

Finally, when I'm about to give up hope, my computer pings. Allie is too lost in her sandwich and TikTok to notice.

The FBI was doing an investigation on his mafia so he has an entire profile. I pull it up and see a picture of the man from last night. Vadim Yegorov. Russian-born, started doing grunt work for the Bratva when he was only a kid and moved his way up until he transferred to New York with his Brigadier—or boss— Mikhail Belov, who was transferred over from his boss—the Pakhan—in Russia. Mikhail and Vadim have been in New York for the past thirteen years. Mikhail is now the Pakhan of the New York Bratva, and Vadim is one of his Brigadiers, and I guess his most trusted one. And I killed him.

Fuck.

This will not be easily swept under the rug. Someone—everyone—will be looking for Vadim. We need to fix this or else the entire Bratva will be gunning for me and the Outlaws.

That fucking disaster aside, why was Vadim tasked with kidnapping Allie though? Why would Mikhail send one of his top guys for something so small? Unless this has something to do with her father, but even if Alexei Lenkov crossed Mikhail, I still think he'd send a lower-ranking soldier to get Allie.

Fuck, there are too many questions and not enough answers right now. I need to dig into Alexei and see if he had anything to do with Mikhail and if he fucked over Mikhail recently. It didn't seem that Vadim was intending to kill Allie, he was trying to take her, so they wanted her alive.

Sighing, I reach down and pull an energy drink from my mini fridge.

"Okay." Allie's voice breaks the silence, and I realize how loud my head was and that the room was actually completely silent. "Let's go for a walk outside. We've both been too attached to screens for a while."

I sigh, not because of Allie, but from pure exhaustion. I've been going on small bursts of sleep for weeks, and I just wish one thing would come easily—that I would get answers the first time I looked into something—but that's not hacking and digging. The people we deal with keep shit locked down tight for a reason, and I enjoy that usually. I like the search and the chase, but right now this is too dire—too close to my heart—to want to search for answers. I want them now. "I've got too much to do, beautiful," I say gently.

Allie comes up behind me and wraps her arms around my neck. "It'll be here later. Come on, let's go clear our heads."

I can't argue with her. Whatever she says, I'll do. "Okay." I close out my screen and Allie stands, allowing me to push away from the desk. She takes my hand and we leave my room together.

I guess I can put off figuring out exactly how dead I am for a few minutes.

24

SAINT

I SPEND THE ENTIRE DRIVE TO MY HOUSE REPLAYING THE conversation between Allie and me. I couldn't look at Mason as I stepped out of the Chapel. I would have buried my thumbs in his eye sockets and smashed his head into the wall until the sound of her voice saying she could love him stopped playing through my mind.

I leave my bike in the driveway and slam the front door closed. I never needed anyone in my life until I came into the club and then met Allie, and now I've lost everyone. And it's worse with Allie because I have to watch her with Mason. To see him standing protectively over her when I should be there. To know he was the one to kill the guy who broke into her house. That should have never happened because she should have been here with me. My boots land on the stairs with loud thunks as I stomp up the stairs and to my room. I need a cold shower. My skin is burning up at the thought of him being in her home, of her being in his bed at the clubhouse, and whatever they're doing now. Living happily without me. Fuck her.

But when I step into my bedroom, all I see is her. All I've seen is the ghost of her since she spent the night. I take a deep breath, hoping to calm myself, but all I smell is her perfume on my sheets, the floral scent clinging to the leather of my cut. I grip the arm and yank it off of one shoulder, letting it fall to the floor, and stare around my room, watching her movements of the night we were together. Joined on the bed, sleeping in each other's arms, her sitting with me while I drew in the morning.

I can't take it anymore. Her ghost is everywhere, haunting me. I take the stupid vase from the dresser and throw it at the wall above the bed, shattering it. And then I lose it. Everything reminds me of her, and I break it all. Fuck her. Fuck her for leaving me when I needed her the most. Fuck her for making me love her when I never wanted to love anyone. Fuck her for choosing one of my brothers and then shoving it down my throat. Fuck Mason for falling for her, though I can't find it in me to blame him—because I fell for her too. I stalk to the bed, step up on it, and jump as hard as I can, breaking the boards under it and causing the mattress to fall through. I kick out the sideboards, and the footboard crashes down. I yank the head-board down and smash it to the ground.

The chair. I saw our future there. Me sitting and drawing as the sun rose and Allie sitting next to me, drinking a coffee, watching the sky and the whales in the water below. I lift the chair and throw it at the dresser, and when that barely does anything to it, I shove it to the floor and stomp on the backside of it, causing it to cave in.

My chest heaves as my breaths come in heavily. I need more. The nightstands are the only things still standing. Yanking the lamps off, the cord breaking with the force, I slam my foot into the front of it, cracking the wood, then repeat that on the other one. One lamp is still in my hand when I turn my head and look into the bathroom and my blood pressure rises even higher, if that's possible. Tossing the lamp and catching it in my hand, I eye the toothbrush that she used that I left on the counter for her. Then I toss the fucking lamp into the mirror and watch the picture of Allie crack and shatter, and that feels pretty fucking fitting considering the current circumstances.

Turning around, I look around my destroyed bedroom. I walk to the dresser—it's really not that broken other than the backing—so I flip it right side up and yank some drawers open, pulling out handfuls of clothes, and then I walk to my bed and pick up my pillow. I carry the clothes and my pillow to one of the spare rooms. I'm leaving Allie and everything I feel for her behind in that room. All of the destruction and pain and rage. She means nothing to me anymore.

25

MASON

"Allie's house is brand new, why did she need to replace the flooring, and why did it need to be this weekend?" Reese asks as she flips through another catalog.

"I'm not sure, Princess," I drawl, looking over her shoulder at the endless couches, chairs, dining room tables, blah, blah, blah. Everything is white and wood and running together in my mind. If it was possible to die of boredom I would have keeled over in the Ski House Collection catalog.

"Thank you for coming with me since Cale is helping Allie." Reese smiles over at me and I can't help it, I smile too. Reese is one of my best friends—my little sister. I love her.

"Anything for you, Princess." I lean over and tuck her under my arm, staring into the book as she flips pages again.

She angles the pages toward me, showing me the newest set in the Beach House Collection. "What about this one?" she asks.

I look over yet another white sectional and warm wood table. "Looks great, really fits you."

Reese narrows her eyes and nods, and I hold in a laugh. "Yeah, that's what I was thinking too, and I think Cale will like it. He said he didn't care how I decorated the house." In my opinion, Cale got off lucky, and fuck him for asking me to come with Reese to pick out furniture for their new house, even though I would have done it anyways. This has been the most boring day of my life!

The sales associate nods as Reese places the book on the table between us. "St. Barts, that's a good choice. Okay, let's go over specific items and rooms now."

Snooze.

We've picked out furniture, lighting fixtures, décor, rugs, and window treatments, and finally—*finally*—Reese stands and shakes the woman's hand. We've been here since morning and it's now lunchtime, and I'm starving.

Reese and I go to lunch at the drive-in I took her to when she was all down on Cale and pretending she didn't love him. I have to bring her back down to earth after the amount she just spent on furniture.

"How's your nose and ribs?" Reese asks, bringing a bite of chili dog to her mouth.

"Well, it's only been about a week," I say, picking up a fry.

The wind blows through the little outdoor eating area where Reese and I are seated. The breeze feels nice on our exposed skin, and the awning over us keeps us out of the hot sun.

"Yeah." She eyes me. "Thanks for keeping the sunglasses on at the appointment. You still look pretty bad."

I think back to the police officers showing up at Allie's house that night. Good thing the lights were low and they couldn't see the full extent of my bruising. A small smile lifts my lips while I roll my eyes. "Thanks, Princess."

Reese chuckles and takes another bite of her food, but after a moment, her smile fades and her brows pull together. "Are you okay? With everything with Saint and Allie?"

I take a sip of my soda to give myself a chance to think, not that I haven't been thinking about all of this since Saint and I happened at Leo's party, but Reese won't take any bullshit from me. She's kind of in the middle here—there's only one person she's closer to than she is to Allie and me, and that's Cale. "I'm fine—" Reese opens her mouth to call me out, but closes it again when I give her a stern look. "I'm fine. Do I wish that there was nothing between them and that she only wanted me? Hell yes. But I know she cares about him a lot, and I care about her, and that makes it hard for me to ask her to give him up. I won't do it, and if I have to share her with his ghost, then so be it. I'll give her all of me until she decides she doesn't want me anymore. But I hope that doesn't happen." I take another drink, my throat getting dry talking about my real thoughts out loud for the first time. "He's gotta stop talking to her like he does though. If he doesn't want her anymore then fine, but he needs to quit making the scars deeper."

"Cale said it was tense between them at church," Reese says softly, biting her lip.

Scoffing, I shake my head. "That's a fucking understatement. He looked like he wanted to bite her head off while he fucked her into the table, and she looked like she wanted to crawl into a hole and hide."

Reese leans forward on the table, speaking lower. "Maybe you guys just need to take it to the next step." She fakes a gag, and I laugh at her theatrics.

"I thought you didn't want to talk about my sex life?" I smirk when she winces.

"I don't, but maybe that's what she needs to get Saint out of her mind." She raises her eyebrows and looks at me intently.

Shaking my head, I run my tongue over my lips. "I don't want to be a rebound for her, Reese. And you know that wouldn't work anyways, you've seen the way she looks at him."

"I didn't mean it like that. You're not a rebound to her, Mase. I've seen the way she looks at you too." She stands and walks to my side of the table. Sliding onto the bench next to me, she leans into my side and I wrap an arm around her shoulder. "I couldn't imagine a better man for her, and I wouldn't want you with anyone else but her. I really want you guys to work out."

I hug her tightly and she snuggles in closer to my side. "Me too, Princess, me too." I want that more than anything.

26

ALLIE

"I THOUGHT YOU SAID WHEN YOU FOUND OUT WHO THAT GUY WAS, that I could go back home." I crawl onto the bed, watching Mason. I want to go home. I like being with Mason, but I just wish we were at my house, where my things are. My favorite mug, my coffee machine, my sheets, my bed, my water pressure. Ugh!

Sighing, he leans back against the pillows that he propped up against the wall. "Are you tired of me already, beautiful?"

I cock my head and pin him with an unamused look. "Be serious, Mase." I realize I used his nickname for the first time after it's already out there, but I don't regret it. I like him. A lot. He makes me feel adored and wanted. He makes me feel safe.

"I did say that, but I still don't know why Vadim was in your house, and I'm not comfortable with you being back there until I know that the threat is over." I recoil at the reminder of the man who attacked me. Mason drags his tan hand down his face and rests his head against the wood-paneled wall.

"Why can't you turn my house into Fort Knox like you did Reese's apartment when she was being stalked?" I get to his side and sit with my legs underneath me, looking down at him.

"Because that's not guaranteed to keep everyone out." I sigh, and he continues, "I promise to get you home as soon as possible, Al."

I drop my shoulders, guilt setting in. Mason has been working nonstop. I have to force him to eat something more than chips or a few bites of a sandwich, or to sleep. I've looked over his shoulder when he thinks I'm not paying attention. I know he's also trying to solve Ronan's murder. He has a lot on his shoulders right now, but he won't stop. He won't give up on trying to save everyone. "I'm sorry, it's just this place—"

"Isn't what you're used to, I know," he says softly. I know what he thinks, *the rich girl is throwing a fit because she's not in her castle.* That's not it, that's not me—at least I try to not let it be me. I like nice things, but I mostly just like *my* things. My dad was always traveling between Russia and New York, and I never got any notice, always just having to pack up and go whenever he said. I don't like change, or being forced to go somewhere. This feels like another trip to Russia in a private jet that was never home. In a brownstone home on a quiet Russian street that was never home. A three-story townhome that was never home. My house in Merrill Hill was the first place that ever felt like home. My dad might have owned it, but I made it my home.

"It's just a little small, and sometimes smells like cheap perfume," I say instead of that I just miss my damn sheets. Mason chuckles and shakes his head. "I'm sorry. I'm not trying to be a spoiled brat." I look down.

"You're not." Mason reaches out his hand, holding it open for me. I place my hand in his and lift my eyes, he looks so exhausted. He gently pulls me toward him. "Come here, let's watch this movie and go to bed. Everything will be better tomorrow." I fall down onto the bed next to him and curl up under his arm. His warmth settles into my bones and calms me immediately, and this place starts to feel a little like home. We watch the movie that's starting on his computer at the end of the bed.

Throughout the movie, I move around, trying to find the most comfortable position, and I finally find it by laying one of my legs over his and resting my head on Mason's bare chest. I get distracted and stare down at his chiseled ab muscles, and without much thought, I lightly trace my finger over them. Mason jolts, the muscles in his stomach tightening more and popping under my finger. I can feel his head move, his chin grazing the top of my head, watching me.

"What are you doing?" Mason's voice is rough and he clears his throat twice.

Licking my lips, I know what I want and I'm going to get it. "Exploring." I trace the waistband of his athletic shorts. "You can explore too if you want."

The hand that was resting beside him moves to my thigh and he lightly grazes it with his fingers, smoothing them back and forth over my skin. I involuntarily moan at how good it feels. I feel tingles where his fingers trace, he feels electric.

"Damnit, Allie," Mason groans and pulls his fingers away.

"No!" I whine, pulling his hand back to my thigh.

Mason lets out a throaty chuckle and strokes my leg again. "I can't be a gentleman when you make noises like that."

Picking up my head, I rest it against his chest and look into his unique eyes. "I don't like gentlemen."

Mason licks his lips and leans forward, his lips brushing mine as he speaks. "Do you want me to touch you, Solnyshko?" Mason calls me 'little sun' in Russian, and my jaw drops. He chuckles, and a warm smile spreads across his face.

"How..." I trail off, surprised that he knows the language.

"I started listening to an app while I'm coding. It's your heritage, I wanted to know about it." He shrugs—as much as one can when they're laying down with a person on top of them —like it's no big deal, but it is.

Leaning forward, I take his bottom lip between mine and suck on it. Mason and I stare at each other. "I want you to touch me, Mason," I whisper when I pull away.

"Where, baby?" he asks. My voice gets caught in my throat when his fingers ghost over my slit through my thin sleep shorts. His arm pins my thigh to his side as it rests over it. "Right here?" He grazes it again. "Or here?" He slides his fingers up my shorts and he circles my clit. I suck in a breath and stare into his eyes. He watches me, trying to fight off a smile and failing. "No, no, not there." He moves my panties to the side and runs his fingers through my wetness, then slowly pushes two fingers inside of me. Moaning, I drop my forehead to his shoulder and turn to face his neck, my breath blowing onto his tan skin and making goosebumps rise with my quickening breaths. "Yeah, that's it, isn't it, beautiful?"

His fingers move inside of me slowly, gently dragging over the spongy spot inside of me and sending sparks flying all the way down to my toes. I start to rock my hips in time with his thrusts, hoping to speed him up or push him deeper and he chuckles, his throat vibrating with the sound. "Someone's eager. Ride my fingers, Solnyshko." Heat floods my stomach and I move my hips faster, not needing to be told twice. "That's right, Allie. Faster," Mason demands, and I comply. I'm on the edge of orgasm, my skin tingling with the first waves of it, and Mason pulls his fingers out.

Lifting my head, I look at his infuriating smirk. "What?"

"I'm not wasting an orgasm on my fingers, I want you to finish on my cock." He pushes his shorts off of his hips and down his legs and I gape at the size of him. *Fuck yes.*

Mason grabs a condom from his bedside drawer and rolls it on. I want to tell him not to, that I have the implant and we don't need it. I know Mason wouldn't risk my health, but the only person I haven't used a condom with was Saint, and right now that's all I have left of him. I want to keep it a little longer.

Mason grips my hips, directing me up and on top of him. When I'm on top, he slides his hands down my thighs to rest on the back of my calves, letting me take complete control. I position him at my opening and I savor the stretch of him as I slowly slide down. He's perfect.

I start to ride Mason, moving my hips forward and back, lifting them on the backward motion, and he grabs my chin gently, pulling my face down to his.

"I waited for you for what feels like forever, and nothing I ever imagined ever came close to the real you." His eyes stare straight into my soul, and I know that I will never be without Mason. He's ingrained himself into my very being, and I love him.

I blink, lost for words. The last thing I want to do is blurt out that I love him right now, so I nod, and he lets go of my chin. I lift back up and continue my movements, picking up speed as I race toward the orgasm I was so close to before.

The orgasm hits me like a freight train. All sound is ripped from my lungs as I stop my hips and drop my head back and let the waves wash over me. I don't even register Mason's soft words as I float back to earth.

"Fucking perfect, Allie. You're fucking perfect," Mason whispers, already sitting up and placing gentle kisses to my neck, his hands roaming my back, pushing my thin tank top up. I look down at him and our hearts lock when our gazes do. I've never experienced anything like this; the intense emotions fill the room and make it hard to breathe. "Take this off." Mason lifts my top higher and I lift my arms, letting him pull it over my head and leave me bare.

He moves one hand to my ass and lifts us, placing me on my

back as he stays seated inside of me. "Can you give me one more, Solnyshko?" he asks, and I nod mutely. I'm incapable of words. I'm a little scared at what I'm feeling and the intensity of it. I've only felt this way once.

Mason holds himself up on one elbow as he positions his fingers over my clit and tweaks it as he hammers into me. His preferred pace is a lot faster than what I was doing when I was on top. He hits a new angle this way—deeper. He feels incredible and before long, I'm barrelling over the edge again, staring into his eyes and moaning his name. It's him and I, and no one else. Not Vadim, not my father, not whatever is going on with the Bratva. It's just Mason and me, and the zinging feeling that is from more than two amazing orgasms. Mason pumps into me two more times before burying himself in deep and stilling. He stares into my eyes, and I know that he felt everything I did.

Mason kisses me slowly, sweeping his tongue into my mouth, and his hand moves to cup my face. He pulls away and uses his hand on my cheek to brush some stray strands of hair off of my face.

"I think I love you, Allie," he whispers, like he's afraid to admit it.

I nod, knowing exactly how he feels. We're the same. "I think I love you too," I say just as softly.

He places one last kiss to my lips before pulling out of me and leaving the bed for the attached bathroom. I roll over, pulling up the sheets and watching him leave. His taut ass and back muscles ripple as he walks. Mason works hard for his body, and I've never had the proper opportunity to appreciate it.

Mason returns and climbs into bed. "Come here, I want to hold you for the rest of the night."

"Hang on." I dodge his outstretched arms and climb out of the bed. "I need to clean up first," I say as I walk to the bathroom.

"Okay, I should probably check in with Miles anyway. I asked him to help with Mikhail Belov." I clench my eyes shut tightly as I walk into the bathroom and close the door. Leaning against it, I try to forget everything with the Russians. Tonight is about Mason and me, and I won't let anything ruin it. Not even the smallest bit of guilt that hit me after Mason left for the bathroom when for a split second I thought of Saint. Nothing is going to ruin this for us.

Finishing in the bathroom, I step out and find Mason at his computer. Figures, I'm probably going to have to bribe him away with more sex. How terrible.

But when he turns to look at me as I step out of the bathroom, his eyes wide and lips pressed into a thin line, I stop in my tracks. "It's bad, Saint. It's really fucking bad."

27

SAINT

Noctem's little head rests on the concrete next to me. Her eyes watch Finn as he rolls around the bike, tinkering with parts, tightening bolts, doing whatever the fuck. "I'm Sick of Trying" by Vaboh plays through the speakers hanging from the high ceiling of Finn's shop.

"You're finishing this quickly," I say, sitting on my own rolling stool, though I'm just watching Finn and drinking beer.

"Yeah, well I figure you and Ronan were treating fixing this thing as a drinking social and he was half blitzed every time you worked on it," he grits through his teeth, tightening a bolt with his arm muscle bulging. I shrug. He's right. The tool drops to the floor with a clang and he turns to me. "Should be done in a week or two."

I push out a deep breath and look over the bike. "I never thought of what I was going to do with it. I never thought we would actually finish it, and if we did, I figured Ro would take it."

Finn nods and stares at the floor. "You can keep it here until you decide."

My phone vibrates in my pocket, and I take it out, seeing Mason's name.

Anger flows through me at his name, but I have to remind myself that I can't hate him. He's my brother, and it's her that betrayed me.

"What's up, brother," I bite out, a little harsher than I wanted, and Finn side-eyes me.

"It's bad, Saint. It's really fucking bad," Mason mutters.

Panic sets in. He could be talking about a thousand fucking things. "What's bad? What's going on?" I shout in my urgency to find out what he's talking about. Finn sits straight up, watching me.

"Allie's dad traded her to Mikhail Belov. That's why he sent Vadim. To get her for their wedding." I hear Allie scream her questions at Mason on the other side of the line and I guess this is the first she's hearing of it as well. My traitorous heart turns to stone in my chest and I think it stops altogether with how badly my chest aches. "She can't go, Saint," Mason whispers.

"I fucking know," I snap. "How did you find out?"

"Miles," he answers, and I can still hear Allie screaming at him.

"Can Miles reach out to Mikhail?" I ask calmly, though my mind feels anything but.

Mason swallows roughly, the sound clear through the line. "I think so."

"Have Miles tell Mikhail that I want a meeting," I say, and Finn's eyes widen.

He sighs loudly, "Saint... I... She..." He can't complete his sentences. My mind is racing, so I'm sure his is too.

"I know, Mase. I won't let anything happen to either of you." I hang up before he can panic anymore. I need to think.

"Why are we meeting with Mikhail?" Finn asks slowly.

"We're not. I am," I answer, my eyes roaming the clean floor, trying to calculate everything in my mind.

Finn scoffs, and his heavy steps stop right in front of me. "If my Prez is going in front of the Bratva, I'm going too!" he shouts.

My eyes snap to his and I stand, not allowing him to intimidate me, though I don't think he's trying to. "You have an Old Lady now, and if Mikhail wants blood for Vadim, then I'm not fucking risking you being there." I glare at him. "I won't risk any of you being there."

Finn shrugs one shoulder, watching me. "Forever an Outlaw. If you won't take me, I'll push for a vote, and then everyone will want to come."

Sighing, I drag my hands down my face. "God fucking dammit."

"Why are we meeting with Mikhail?" Finn asks again.

I have to look away from him as my stomach turns, making me nauseous. "Allie's father married her off to Mikhail."

"And Mason killed Vadim. Fuck," Finn whispers, his eyes drifting off.

"Yeah." We're so fucked. We have his 'wife'—like I'll fucking let that happen—and we killed his second in command. We have nothing to go in there with to make demands.

"What are we going to do, Prez?" Finn doesn't ask with resignation, but with trusting confidence in his voice. Finn would follow me over a cliff if I thought it was best for the club, all of my brothers would. They trust me to make the right decisions for the club. To keep them safe and money coming in steadily. I still don't think I'm cut out for this, that I was the one that should have been promoted. "I don't know yet," I finally answer. But I'll do anything to make sure Allie and Mason stay safe right here in Merrill Hill.

Even if it means sacrificing myself to the Bratva boss.

28

SAINT

My brothers slowly filter into the Chapel while I lift the joint to my lips and light the end. I don't smoke often, but so much shit has been consuming my mind, every fucking day is a goddamn struggle, and now all of this shit with Allie and the Bratva is just making things worse. Tobi is the last one to step inside, shutting the door behind him.

"Motherfucking cocksucker!" Finn bellows and all eyes snap to him. He looks up from his phone, his eyes wide when he notices everyone looking at him. He clears his throat, slouching in his chair like that'll hide his giant ass. "Shit, sorry," he mumbles.

"You fucking good?" I ask, looking at him like he's fucking insane.

He tosses his phone onto the table, crossing his thick arms over his wide chest. "Yeah. Huntley just shot down my last ship in Battleship." His phone lights up and he looks down at it, shaking his head with a ghost of a smile. "And now she's talking shit."

Looking away from him, I focus on the real problems we

have instead. "Anyways, Mason, did Miles get in touch with Mikhail?"

Mason stops running his hand through his brown hair for the tenth time since sitting down, and he glances at the door before looking back at me. "You told Allie we weren't discussing this right now, she'll—"

"Allison doesn't run my fucking club, and it's about goddamn time she realized that!" I snap. "If I want her in my fucking Chapel, I'll allow her in. This doesn't concern her right now."

"But it's about her!" Mason challenges.

I'm seething, about to kick his ass out too for arguing with me without hearing any reason. "And it also includes my club!" I shout. "The last thing I need is your girlfriend going behind our backs to sacrifice herself to try to save you." I stub the joint out in the ashtray and scrub my hand over my mouth in an attempt to cool my temper.

Mason looks down at the table. "Yes, Prez."

"Did Miles set a meet with Mikhail?" I ask again, my anger tempered for now. I'm not sure it'll ever be completely gone until I get Allie out of my head.

He looks at me, the stubborn fight having left his eyes. This is what I do best: act rationally and without emotion. I do it so well that people think I don't have any emotions, and most of the time they're right. "Yes. Mikhail is in Russia and he won't be back until next week, but he agreed to meet with you."

"Does he know the reason for the meeting?" I ask, ignoring the questioning stares from around the table. Mason shakes his head quietly.

"Care to share what's going on, Prez?" Nate asks.

I look around at my men—my brothers—and sigh. Not fucking really. The last thing I want to do is bring this to them, to worry them, to lay another thing on their plate. "Alexei Lenkov traded Allie to Mikhail Belov, which is why Vadim was here to get her. Finn and I are going to meet with him to talk through shit and see if we can work something out." Looks are exchanged around the table, and before anyone can butt in, I finish, "And the rest of you are staying here. I don't need to worry about more than Finn and myself. That is not up for discussion."

Arguments ensue, as I knew they would.

"You can't go alone!" Nate yells.

"That's bullshit, there's no way I'm letting you two walk into a fucking ambush," Cale seethes.

"This is fucking stupid." Leo shakes his head.

"No." Jack glares.

"Over my dead fucking body are you going without us," Tobi shouts.

They're all right, this is a terrible fucking idea, but what other option is there? Hand over Allie and Mason? Mikhail will kill Mason and then take Allie to Russia and marry her ass, willingly or not. No. Not an option.

Mason clears his throat and every eye turns to him. "I should be the one going with you, Prez." He holds his head high, his jaw flexing as he stares me down.

"Absolutely not." I shake my head, disregarding him.

"But it's my fault we're in this position in the first place!" he argues.

"Exactly!" I shout, slamming my hand down on the table. "And the minute Mikhail finds out who you are he will kill you. I'm not bringing your body back to Allie, so you'll stay here and make sure neither of you fuck up this plan!" I take a few deep breaths, while everyone stares around the table at each other. I don't lose my cool. Ever. they're not used to seeing this side of me. "We'll send up a drone before we get to the meet that Mason can monitor, and if we don't walk out, you can call the mother chapter and go from there," I say a lot more calmly, looking at my brothers sternly, letting them know this is not up for negotiation. "But I'm going, and Finn is the only one I'm allowing with me. There's no vote. That's it."

Some sigh, some shake their head scowling, others grunt with displeasure, but I'm the President of this club and what I say is law. We don't do this often—an overruling decision—but sometimes it's necessary.

"What are you going to do?" Cale asks quietly.

"Tell him about Vadim, that he should have looked into Allie better before sending someone in for her. She's property of the club, she's not going anywhere, and her father doesn't decide that for her." I avoid Mason's eyes as they snap to mine. He hasn't brought up claiming her, and I won't bring it up to him. He'll have to grow his adult balls and come talk to me about it like everyone else. We don't take votes for Old Ladies, but we do bring it up to the club so everyone knows. Regardless of being officially claimed, everyone knows she's property of the Outlaws.

"And what if he doesn't like that? What if he wants Allie and Mason's blood for Vadim?" Tobi asks across from me.

I can't tell them that I'm not planning to walk out of that meeting. I'm not only bringing Finn because he's my VP and former Enforcer, but also because he'll understand that I'd die for Allie and Mason. Just as he'd die for Huntley and the club. Instead, I say, "I talked to Riz. The Mother Chapter is behind us, so we hope that Mikhail doesn't want to take on the entire Devil's Outlaws, international and stateside."

Everyone looks around the table silently, and I know that they want to argue, to figure out a different plan, but there isn't anything else to do. This is it. I look at each of my brothers, just in case it's the last time I sit in this chair. I have something Ronan didn't have—a warning.

Cale, with his blonde hair and gray-blue eyes, looks between Finn and me. This will be the hardest for him.

Mason shifts in his chair, his eyes darting from everyone to the table, to the door. He's conflicted, I get it.

Wyatt looks like he's tired of life. His beard has grown, and his dark brown hair is longer. He kind of looks like a biker Jesus. He hasn't been the same since Ro died. He's so fucking over it and I can't blame him.

Tobi. Old motherfucker. Not really, but it's fun to taunt him. It'll suck that he'll have survived three club Presidents.

Nate is scowling at me, but I know it's only because he wants to do more. He's always been all in for the club, probably why he never settled down.

Jack stares ahead of him, at the wall above Mason's head. His blonde hair hangs in his eyes. The kid's got demons living inside of him, and I know he struggles with that shit.

Leo actually looks worried for once in his goddamn life. He treats every day like a party, but when it comes down to it, he's always there. It's a little sobering to see this side of him.

Lastly, Finn. His deep blue eyes are hard, and I know I can't talk him out of going, but fuck I wish I could. If something happens to Finn, Huntley will make me wish I was dead.

"Call the girls, get a party going. We need to blow off some steam, and we still haven't celebrated Cale and Reese's bachelor and bachelorette party." I bang the gavel on the table and everyone stands, starting toward the door. "Mason," I call out to him before he leaves. "Don't say a word to Allie about this until it's over."

He dips his head in acknowledgment. "Got it, Prez." Then he follows everyone else out of the chapel, the music picking up in the main room. I look around at the empty chairs one last time before leaving to spend the night with my brothers.

29

ALLIE

ALL OF THE GUYS WALK OUT OF THE CHAPEL, AND MASON LOOKS around before his eyes land on me at the bar. He flashes me a half smile as he walks over. I ended up here when Saint kicked me out of Church and swore they weren't going to be discussing my... situation with my dad and some Russian mobster I'd never met.

"All good?" I ask when he slides onto a barstool next to me.

"All good, just club stuff." His smile falters, but then he turns away and accepts a beer from one of the other members—Nate, I think. "We're gonna have a party tonight, do you want to stay down here, or hide out in my room?"

I've only been to a few club parties, and only because Reese has invited me. "Is Reese coming?" I don't think I'd have a whole lot of fun without her. Yeah, I'd have Mason, but I'd miss my girl too.

Mason smirks. "All of her favorite people in the world are here, so I'm sure she could be convinced," he chuckles, and the off mood he was giving off when he sat down evaporates.

The party picks up quickly. Club girls and the guys fill giant barrels with drinks, and Nate taps a few kegs in the parking lot.

People filter in and soon the clubhouse is stuffy with people and noise. Cale left to go get Reese, and Mason and I stayed at the bar that is now crowded with people asking for drinks and girls running back and forth, getting drinks, and chatting with people. All of the tables that are haphazardly placed around the room are filled, a game is going on at the pool table, and music has started in the strip club at the back of the clubhouse. I haven't seen Saint once, though I know he must be here.

"Come on, let's get out of here and get some fresh air," Mason yells over the music.

I nod my agreement and he takes my hand, directing us out of the clubhouse and into the fresh air, which feels cool compared to the heat of all of the bodies inside. There are a few tables set up outside with people lounging around them, string lights hung up to add some light, and a few tall industrial lights to light the whole compound. There is a boxing ring set up off to the side, and that's where Mason is leading us to.

We pass the tables, and my heart rate picks up. Saint is sitting at one of the tables with Wyatt, Finn, Huntley, and the new Prospect, Nox. He glares at me the entire way past him and when my back is to him, I can still feel his hateful stare on me.

Leo and Jack are in the ring, taking shots at each other and laughing when one lands. Nate and Tobi stand on the side, yelling orders and directions at the guys, and we walk up to them as they trade money between them.

"Told you Jack would be the first one to bleed. Leo is a savage, he'll be our next Enforcer." Tobi grins, pocketing Nate's money.

"I don't know, there's something about J. He's a silent killer. Sneak in and slit your throat while you sleep type of shit." Nate watches on, his eyes narrowed as he assesses the guys closely.

When did these types of conversations become normal to me? I don't believe that the law is always right; it didn't help

Reese at all, and they wouldn't have until it was too late. From the small snippets I've gotten from Reese and Huntley, she was failed by the law as well, but I wonder how well I'll do arguing the law when I don't believe in it. I'm an accessory to murder now, what kind of lawyer does that? Or maybe I don't even want to be a lawyer at all. I chose it because of my dad, because he wanted me to fall in his footsteps, but now I'm figuring everything out. What kind of a scumbag he is.

He *traded me* to a Russian mob boss. Someone who is even more immoral than him. Someone like Mason and Saint.

Fuck.

I can't judge Mikhail for what he's done in his job, only that he accepted a traded bride without her consent. That he was willing to kidnap me and bring me to him to marry me against my will.

But my dad.

He sold his only daughter and for what? We still don't know, and I can't bring myself to ask him. I'm too afraid that he'll realize he fucked up and take more extreme measures to deliver me to Mikhail, or that I might be the next one to take a life.

His life.

He's always been cold towards me. My mother was absent all of the time, and my dad took the role of primary caretaker. And by 'primary caretaker,' I mean he kept me and two nannies with him. He never raised me, neither of my parents did. But I never expected this. What the fuck kind of parent does this? I wonder if my mother knows, or if she'd even care? I'd never reach out to her though.

"Hey, you okay?" Mason asks, looking down at me.

I startle out of my thoughts, realizing that I'm squeezing Mason's hand that's still entwined in mine. "Yeah." I plaster on a smile, but I don't feel like partying anymore. I just want to catch my bestie up and stuff my face with pasta and curl up in bed with Mason. "I just need a drink," I say though because the tiny indentation in between Mason's brow has finally eased and I can tell he's having a good time laughing at Leo and Jack. I'll wait until Reese gets here and then we can sneak away and discuss how fucked my life has gotten in the last month.

Damn, these Outlaws bring havoc, but they also bring the most happiness I've ever known.

Mason steps away, heading to a cooler tank and then bringing us both back drinks. He places his arm over my shoulder and I lean into him, snuggling closer to his side.

The music immediately cuts, all sounds halting as everyone stops talking, and Mason and I look over our shoulders. My eyes fall on Saint as he messes with his phone and then as a song begins, he sets his phone on the table in front of him and continues glaring at me. "Girls Like U" by Blackbear is his song choice, and as I listen to the lyrics, I want to strangle his petty ass.

Reese and Cale finally pull into the parking lot on Cale's bike, saving Saint from me wrapping my hands around his throat and digging my nails in, and not in a sexy way.

Reese beelines to me and gives me a tight hug, and I hang on like my life depends on it. I really need my girl right now.

Reese pulls away from me, her perfect eyebrows pulled together. "What's wrong?" I look around. I don't want to just spill everything right here. Reese picks up on how uncomfortable I am—of course, she does, she's my best friend—and turns to Cale. "Are there any chairs around or something?" He nods and pulls Mason away to bring us chairs.

We're set up off to the side of the boxing ring, random people in there now, and Mason, Cale, Jack, and Leo are standing by, watching the fights. I tell Reese everything. Saint, the break-in, my dad. I couldn't hold anything back from her even if I wanted to, it just pours out, and she doesn't look scared or horrified, she just pulls me into her chest, her soft tee shirt rubbing against my cheek and her musky perfume filling my nose. "The guys will figure this out, Al. You know they will, you're family."

"I just don't know what to think, Reese. My dad..." I trail off, I can't even say it. I'm so tired of even just thinking about it.

"Your dad has always thought of only himself. I'm not excusing his actions, he should pay for this, but I always expected him to marry you off to someone. I just thought it would be a billionaire that he could make a connection with," she says hesitantly, but still confidently.

I bite my lip, thinking it over. She's right. It does sound like something he would do. Not be connected to the Bratva and trade me off to him, but to force a relationship with someone that would benefit him.

"Has the club figured out what they're going to do about it?" Reese asks.

I shake my head. "No, but Saint said I could be in Church when they did."

Reese's eyebrows raise. "Wow. I was never a part of any of the meetings about my stalker."

I shrug one shoulder. "I'm more assertive. I walked into the Chapel without an invitation."

She smirks, her brick-red lips sliding into a smile. "Yeah well, banging the President gets you a different set of rules." Then she cackles when my mouth drops open.

"We're not *banging* anymore," I stress the word she used. "Now I just want to bang his head against the wall and I'm pretty sure he wished I didn't exist."

Reese looks behind me, at the table where Saint is sitting. I made sure to take the seat that would have my back to him if I turned to face Reese, that way I didn't have to look at him. It hurts to see how much he hates me now.

"Just say the word and I'll kill him, Al. I don't care about the club or any of this shit. I've been taking lessons with Huntley, and she's taught me some stuff." Reese wiggles her brows at me.

"Calm down, killer." We laugh loudly at each other, the guys turning to cast looks at us before focusing back on their conversation.

I stay with Reese at the chairs, Mason and Cale making sure our drinks never go empty, and after a while, I'm regretting taking them. My voice is louder, and Reese and I laugh a lot more than necessary at the things we're saying, and I even chance glances back at Saint. Every time he's glaring at me.

After the third time, I tell myself that I'm not turning around anymore. With how many drinks I've had, I might start crying, and I am not a drunk crier.

But as Reese's eyes widen and then turn to slits, her pouty lips press into a thin line. Oh no, nope. What the fuck is Callum doing? I'll kill him if he hurts my bestie.

I whip around, my hair flying around me as I turn my body to see what she's looking at, but it isn't her biker that's causing that look on her face, it's mine. Or fuck, not mine. Saint.

It's Saint, sitting in the stupid chair where he has a perfect line of sight right to me, with a tipsy, dark-haired girl. She's only wearing a bra and denim shorts, her perky tits pushed up to her fucking chin, and Saint looks up at her, talking to her.

I see red.

Standing, my wine cooler falls to the concrete, the glass cracking as it lands, and I hear Reese call my name as I stalk toward the table. I don't listen to her, not when she calls my name again, and not when Mason does. I just watch Saint say something to her, and she giggles.

Her high-pitched laugh rings around in my head, and it just enrages me more. My feet pick up into a run, my sandals clacking against the concrete, and everyone at the table turns to see what the noise is.

No one stops me, and when I reach Saint's side, I grab the girl by her hair and pull her off of him. Her knees hit the ground and her hands reach up to wrap around my hand while she screams. I drag her a few paces away—I'm not strong enough to do anything cooler—and I lean down, noticing the bright red scrape marks on her knees, blood slipping through the cuts. Oops.

"Don't ever sit on his lap again. Do you hear me? Next time I won't be so gentle," I hiss into her face while she glares at me. I release my tight grip on her hair, pushing her head forward when I let go.

"You're not his Old Lady," she snaps at me. "Saint, tell this dumb whore to fuck off." She turns around, still on her knees, to look at him, and I look up from where I'm crouched. Oh my God, please don't say something mean that will embarrass me in front of all of these people staring. My stupid jealousy caused everyone to stop what they were doing and turn to watch us. The entire parking lot is watching. Why did I do this? I've never been a jealous girlfriend, or person, whatever. I'm not going to try to deny that I still want Saint and that there is still something there.

He watches us, his eyes flicking between us as he slowly brings a lighter and cigarette to his lips and lights it. I'm going to die. He inhales and releases the smoke. "You heard her, Jillian, get the fuck out of my clubhouse."

Standing, I glare down at the girl, waiting for her to get up and walk her trashy ass out of here. She may not be trashy—she might be lovely—but right now I hate her.

Jillian stands, her hateful glare staying on me the whole way up, and if looks could kill I'd be dust. She spits at my feet, luckily not landing on my foot but next to it. How gross would that be? "Cunt," she hisses.

Taking a couple steps back from her, I shrug and then motion for the gates. "Bye, Vivian." I purposely mess up her name.

Jillian's face twists into a sneer and she rears her fist back, about to launch it at my face, but before she can, Huntley steps in between us, towering over the both of us.

"I know you know who the fuck I am, and unless you want *me* to beat your ass, I'd do as Saint said and get the fuck out." Huntley's smooth voice is calm. Her beautiful tone sounds odd against her threats, but that's who she is. A beautiful voice for an insanely beautiful woman. Jillian doesn't move. "I beg you to try me." Huntley drops her hands to her side.

Jillian releases an angry-sounding breath and walks away, glaring at all of us.

When Jillian is far enough away and stomping toward her car, Huntley turns to walk to the table. "Huntley," I say, and she stops, turning to me. "You didn't need to... shit, I'm sorry. I don't know why I did that," I whisper. I don't want anyone at the table to hear me admit that. And by anyone, I mean Saint.

Huntley smiles a wicked smile, and it would terrify me if I knew she wasn't just as sweet. "That's the most fun that I've had tonight. I wish she would have taken that swing." A laugh bursts out of me before I can stop it and I slap my hand over my mouth to cover any more. The confrontation didn't dampen my buzz at all.

I turn at the sound of Jillian speeding out of the compound and when I turn back around to walk away—because what else do I do after I just pulled a girl by her hair to the ground—I walk right into Saint's chest.

His hands clamp around my shoulder, keeping me pressed against him. "What the fuck was that?" he snaps.

"Do you want her?" I hiss, my voice rising. My blood boils at the thought of her wrapping her legs around him. Would he take her to the Chapel? To his house? Would he buy her pizza? Ask her to wear nothing but his cut? I can feel the rage course through my blood again, and my hands start to tremble.

"No, but why can't I? You're flaunting Mason in front of me all night. Why can't I be with someone else?" he yells.

What do I say? Because I want you, you stupid fuck? Because every night I wish you were with me too? Because although I have Mason, I still yearn for you? I don't know what to say, so I just scream instead. An angry, frustrated scream, and jerk out of his hold. I want to hit him right in his angry, smug face. I turn around and walk to the door of the clubhouse. I need to get out of here, I'm tired of people watching us blow up at eachother and I need to fucking breathe without Saint's presence choking me.

"Fucking brat," Saint sighs.

I want to turn around to yell at him more, but I keep walking, people stepping out of my way as I storm out of the parking lot and into the clubhouse. "Make up sex" by Machine Gun Kelly and Blackbear plays loudly through the clubhouse. I push my way through the throng of people and banging on the bathroom door at the far end of the room.

A man yanks open the door and stares at me as he steps out, probably wondering why I'm slamming my fist on the door like a rude, crazy person. I step inside and slam the door behind me, but when I don't hear it shut, I spin around, thinking the man decided he would come in here with me.

I don't know if it's better or worse when I turn around and see Saint.

30

ALLIE

He flicks the lock on the door and turns to face me. His blonde hair hangs in his glass eyes as he cocks his head and runs his eyes down my body. I didn't realize how drunk he was when we were outside, but I can see it clearly in his bleary eyes now.

It doesn't show in the way he moves though. He closes the gap between us, pushing me into the wall with his chest. I can feel his heat melting through my clothes and into my body, and I crave him.

His hands hover over my hips as he stares at them. Indecision in his eyes.

"Touch me," I whisper. So quiet, it's almost inaudible. I'm too afraid to break the moment.

"Where?" Saint croaks, his voice rough, and he clears his throat.

I take his hands and press them into my hips, sliding them slightly under the loose black tank top I'm wearing, while I raise my hips and press them into his thighs. "Kiss me." I incline my head, presenting my lips to him.

"Do me a favor." He leans in, his lips brushing against mine. His voice skitters over my skin, raising goosebumps in its wake.

"Anything," I whisper, closing my eyes. I'd do anything for this man, absolutely anything for his touch. For his hands gripping me, his heart wrapped around mine tighter than his arms when we fucked on the table in the Chapel.

"Move." Saint shoves me off of him, turning around sharply and stalking to the door.

The absence of his heat hits me harder than a train, and I break. All of the emotions I've been holding back from him come to the surface at once. "No," my voice cracks on the sob as my back slides down the wall and my knees hit the cold tiled floor.

I hear Saint's steps stop, and then they come back to me, but I don't pick my head up. I continue to stare at the white and gray tile with tears spilling down my cheeks. His white Air Forces come into my blurry vision, and then his hand wraps around my chin and lifts my face to look at him.

"If I fuck you, it's over for you. No other man will ever touch you again. You can say goodbye to Mason because if he ever looks at you again, I will slit his throat and fuck you while he bleeds out." Though glassy, I don't see any emotion in Saint's eyes. I can't gauge how he feels.

I shake my head, his hand falling from my chin. "No."

Saint's hands slap into the wall on both sides of me, and he leans down over me. "I don't give a fuck if he's a brother, you're my Queen and nobody fucks with what's mine."

My eyes narrow at him. How can one man take me from devastated to enraged in a nanosecond? "I'm not just yours, Saint. I'll fuck who I want, where I want, how I want, and if you keep trying to piss on me—"

Saint's lips slam onto mine, cutting off my sentence. He bites at my lips and then traces his tongue over them when little whimpers leave me. He pulls away, gripping the backs of my thighs roughly as he lifts me from the floor. "You are mine, Allison." My arms wrap around his shoulders so I don't fall, and then he drops my ass onto the bathroom counter, his big body crowding mine again. "You always have been." He kisses me again, his tongue sweeping in to claim me. As if he ever left. He pulls away. "You always will be," he says as he pulls me off of the counter by my hips and turns me around so my back is against his chest. "Remember when you said you loved me?" His breath tickles my neck as he nibbles along the column.

I stretch my neck so he has more room, loving the little bites he's placing on my skin. "That's not what I said," I moan.

"But that's what you meant." His hand slowly moves down my stomach. "I do too." He flicks the button on my jeans and pushes them over my hips with my panties. My mind comes online at his admission, and my eyes snap to his in the large mirror over the sink in front of us. He's already watching me, his eyes pinning me in my place. "Remember that, because I'm about to fuck you like I hate you." And then he shoves his dick inside of me without any warning. I didn't even realize his jeans were down, but my hips slam into the sink. The impact on the corner splits the skin there and sends a jolt of pain through my body, but it's dulled by the relentless power of Saint's hips behind me. I can't seem to care. This is what I wanted. I wanted him again. Inside of me, our hearts coming together as much as our bodies.

One of his hands reaches up and wraps around my throat, holding me still against him and looking straight into the mirror.

"Look at what I do to you. Watch how you fall apart for me," he says into my ear. His hips pick up more speed and my hips bounce off of the counter and back into him with every thrust. His hand tightens around my throat and I can see his eyes flare in the mirror. "Does he do this to you?" he snaps. His other hand falls between me and the counter and his long fingers start to tease my clit. "Do you see what you do to me, baby? You make me fucking crazy." He presses harder, his finger rubbing rough circles around my clit and I start to lock up around him, my orgasm coming quickly. Everything falls away from me and it's just us. The party, outside, the girl on his lap, the fact that we're in a bathroom and I don't know how clean it is. All of it is gone and it's just us.

I cum. I cum so hard. Saint lets go of my throat, letting me scream his name as my pussy squeezes his dick. I can feel his cock thickening inside of me, but Saint doesn't slow, he pounds into me harder, and my body bends with the exhaustion of my orgasm, my chest falling onto the counter in front of me, and Saint follows me down as he stills inside of me. "It's only ever been you," he whispers, and I relish the weight of his body on mine as he lays over me, both of us breathing heavily.

Saint stands, pulling out of me and pulling up his jeans with a word. Lifting my head, I watch him in the mirror. He looks me in the eyes before stepping away. "Go back to Mason, Allison." His voice is cold again and a fresh bout of tears fills my eyes.

Pushing off of the counter, I pull up my shorts and button them. Saint watches me in the mirror, and when my shorts are secured, he pockets his phone and flips the lock, and opens the door. Taking half of my heart with him.

The reality of what just happened sets in. Did I just cheat on Mason? Groaning, I wipe the tears from my eyes and leave the bathroom.

I walk through the clubhouse with my head down. I have to talk to Mason. God, I hope he won't hate me.

If I lose them both I think I'll die.

Me crashing into a solid body causes me to finally lift my head, and as some stroke of fucking misfortune, it's Saint. He spins around, and his hand clamps around my mouth, his other hand cradling the back of my head as he looks down at me with panicked eyes. I blink up at him, not moving or attempting to say anything.

"Go to Mason's room and lock the door," Saint snaps. "Now!" He pushes me away from him, turning me around in the direction of the stairs.

I stumble forward and look over my shoulder out of the door and see a swarm of bikers standing outside, but they're not a part of this club. One has his back turned and his patch says *Kings of Mayhem*. My feet carry me, but I keep looking over my shoulder as Saint steps through the door and starts walking toward the new guys. One makes eye contact with me, his head cocked and a creepy smile on his face.

I quickly turn around and run for the stairs. I don't have a good feeling about this.

31

MASON

THE CRACKING OF GLASS ON CONCRETE BREAKS CALE'S AND MY conversation, and we both turn our heads toward the sound. Allie is on her feet, and I follow her angry steps to Saint and see one of the cut sluts sitting on his lap. Then Allie starts running for them.

Ah, fuck. I shove my beer bottle into Cale's chest, letting him take it from me as I move to intervene, but I only get a few steps before Allie is yanking the girl by her hair to the ground and I hold in a snort.

Hell yeah. I love watching her stick up for herself and give Saint some shit back after everything he's been saying to her.

Reese joins me in watching Allie lean down and talk to Jillian. "Should we step in?" I ask, watching the show.

"No," Reese says calmly. "Let her handle this."

Jillian stands, cocks her hand back, and Reese and I start moving toward them. This bitch is not laying a hand on Allie— not with the both of us here—but Huntley steps into the mix, standing between them and saying something to Jillian which causes her face to screw up, and then she turns to storm away.

Saint stands, and I hold my breath. What the fuck is he going to do this time, and why do I keep letting him do shit to her?

They share heated words, and Allie screams before stomping off, but when I go to follow, Reese grabs my arm, inclining her head toward Saint, who is going after Allie. "Let them work this out, or let him finally put the final nail in his coffin."

As much as I hate it, she's right. This shit swirling between them is toxic and it's just going to keep going until one of them puts it out of its misery, but it has to be them. I can't do that, no matter how much I wish I could.

I sit in the chair that Allie abandoned and wait for Saint and Allie to come back—mainly Allie—and it feels like a lifetime that they are inside the clubhouse talking.

I'm about to go in and check on them—I don't care what Reese said—when a roar of bike engines split the night air. Every brother is here, who else would be coming to the compound? Thirteen bikes roll through the open gates, and I immediately regret our decision to leave them open. Prospects usually man the gates for the first few hours and then we stop letting people in. This time, we just left them open since we only have Nox.

Every member stands, our hackles rising. We know exactly who these guys are. Cale and I create a wall out of our bodies and he shoves Reese behind us. Leo stalks over to Huntley, still shirtless from his fight and wiping the sweat from his face with his shirt. He takes her from Finn, though she's putting up a fight.

Jack, Nate, and Tobi walk over to Finn and Nox, standing with them. Cale gives me a look and I nod, knowing exactly what he's thinking. Turning around, I grab Reese and gently pull her so she'll walk with me. Thankfully she does without any arguing, and I think she's confused.

"Stay with Huntley and go find Allie, please," I say to her

quietly, trying to block her body with mine while I walk her toward Leo and Huntley.

"What's going on, Mase?" Reese sounds panicked, and I don't blame her. We're literally carting the women out of here to go hide in the clubhouse.

"Cale will tell you later, just go find Allie and stay somewhere with a lock. One of the bedrooms upstairs." I look down at her, and she tries to look over her shoulder, but Cale is already gone to stand with Finn and the rest of the club. Leo waits at the door to the clubhouse with Saint. No Allie. My heart sinks, but I maneuver Reese in front of me and push her forward. "Go, find her." Reese looks at me over her shoulder and nods, walking into the clubhouse without another word.

"She's in Mason's room," Saint says as she passes and she glares at him before walking through and linking her arm with Huntley's. I open my mouth to ask what the fuck happened, but before I can, Saint snaps, "Later," as he walks past me.

Leo falls into step behind him and motions his head forward for me to follow with them.

The Kings of Mayhem have already stepped off of their bikes and are standing around our parking lot, eyeing the club sluts that are scurrying inside. Leo stops to lead them.

"You guys didn't invite us to your party?" Skull, the President of the Kings, asks. His real name is Ian Moore. His eyes roam over the compound and everyone here. Fuck, I hope he didn't get a good look at Huntley or Reese. I hope none of them did.

"Why would we do that?" Saint cocks his head, staring straight at the bald motherfucker.

"We're friends," Colter, the King's VP, drawls.

"Since fucking when?" Nate snaps, and Saint turns his head to glare at him to shut up.

Leo, Jack, Nox, Wyatt, and I stand by, but we watch the interaction closely. None of us were around for what went down between the Outlaws and the Kings. Jack and I weren't even in the city at the time. I don't think Nox was either.

"Since he killed our Prez, and Skull had to come to an agreement with your scumbag asses." Colter steps toward Nate but glares at Finn.

Finn's eyes narrow at Colter, his blue eyes deepening, but he stays silent. Finn would crush Colter, but he could probably take on Nate, so I guess he's choosing his battles.

"And *you* killed my best fucking friend," Nate snarls.

A slow smirk spreads across Colter's face and a mocking laugh rumbles up his throat. "Yeah, I think I remember him."

Nate sucks in an audible breath, and I know shit is about to hit the fan.

"Knock it the fuck off, both of you!" Saint snaps. "Get control of your lap dog, Skull. The peace pact was not President specific, so what the fuck are you doing at my clubhouse uninvited?"

Skull chuckles like this is all so funny, but the tension in the air is thick. Every man in this parking lot is sporting glares and snarling lips. There might be peace between us, but there is no shortage of hatred. I read the police reports, the coroner's reports, and the news articles. This was a statewide war, and if it had continued, there wouldn't have been a victor. The clubs would have wiped each other out, leaving no one behind. Finn ended it by taking out the King's President. He was the one who was behind the war to begin with.

"Back off, Colt. We're just here to make sure the Outlaws remember the stipulations of the pact." He doesn't take his cold stare off of Saint.

"I don't know what there is to forget. You stay on your side of the state, we stay on ours." Saint glares right back, and this time I'm glad he has such a ruthless stare, and that it's not pointed at my girl.

Skull cracks his neck, a false show of relaxation, but I can see his tense shoulders. He's just as ready to jump as the rest of us are. "I got reports the Outlaws are stepping into dust."

Saint scoffs and crosses his arms, and Skull eyes him closely. "We don't fuck around with blow."

"Oh yeah? I heard you were stepping into the weed business." Fucking Colter won't shut his mouth.

Saint casts a fleeting, bored look over Colter before facing Skull again. "Your pocket VP is below me and I won't answer to him. You got something to ask me, do it."

"So it's true?" Skull asks, ignoring Colter's angry face and heavy breathing. He's a mouth breather. Gag.

"Marijuana and cocaine are two very different things, and weed wasn't in our agreement. So if we want to, then yeah, we will."

Skull narrows his eyes and nods slowly. "Okay, well just remember, if anyone breaks the agreement, the pact is off."

Saint smiles and leans forward into Skull's face, causing Finn to stiffen at his side. "I think it would do *you* well to remember. You're the one in our territory uninvited." Straightening, he drops the mean smile. "This could have been a phone call. Don't ever come to my clubhouse again, and I better not find any of you in Merrill Hill without a call first."

Skull slaps Saint on the shoulder, and Saint lifts his top lip in disgust at the gesture. "Got it. Glad we cleared that up."

"Get the fuck out of our clubhouse," Finn grunts.

Colter smirks, piping up again. "We were sorry to hear about your President."

Saint, Finn, and Cale all lunge toward Colter, but Saint makes it to him first, the other two backing off when Saint's hands wrap around Colter's throat and he squeezes. "Don't get this confused, motherfucker. I would kill and die for that man, and if you ever speak his name, no peace pact will stop me. I will kill you with my bare hands, regardless of any consequences." Saint stands over Colter, his fingers digging into his skin. "Don't. Ever. Speak. Of him. Again." Saint punctuates the words by slowly squeezing harder. Still holding onto a red Colter, Saint looks at Skull. "You have a disrespectful VP." He shoves Colter away from him by his throat, and he falls into another of their glaring members, coughing and spluttering. His hands wrap around his own throat as he glares at Saint. "Get out. Now," Saint snaps, and after a brief stare down, the Kings finally start to turn to return to their bikes, Colter spitting on the ground before he leaves with his brothers.

Skull turns around at the last minute, his eyes landing on Nox. "Do you know who you're prospecting for, Prospect? What this club did?"

Straightfaced, Nox answers, "I know exactly who my club is."

Nodding, Skull bites the edge of his lip and turns to follow his club.

The second the last tail light is out of the compound, Jack, Leo, Wyatt, Nox, and Tobi are rushing to the gate to close it. Cale, Finn, and I are rushing for the clubhouse. Finn is running, and this would be a fun time to make fun of him for being whipped if I weren't two steps behind him, moving just as fast. The Kings of Mayhem are disgusting. Their main gig is cocaine, but it's been rumored that they've been dabbling in prostitution and even started dipping their toes in trafficking. That's one of the reasons we sent the girls inside. That, and they are just assholes and we didn't want the girls caught in any crossfire.

"My room, I think," I call to Finn.

Our feet sound like thunder on the stairs as we take them three at a time.

Finn pounds on my door, if he were any harder his fist would go through the wood. "Open up, Angel!" Finn shouts.

The door swings open, and Huntley stands there, pointing a gun out, but Finn takes it from her and pulls her into him. "Jesus, Finn, what's going on?"

Cale pushes between them and the doorframe, barging his way into the room, and I follow him. Reese and Allie are sitting on the bed with Allie's legs tucked underneath her and holding hands with Reese.

"At home, Angel," Finn says into Huntley's hair as he pulls her out of the room.

Cale kneels in front of Reese, who keeps hold of Allie's hand. Allie won't look at me.

"Who were those guys?" Reese asks, linking her free hand in Cale's.

"Another club that we had some problems with a few years ago. They were just here making sure we weren't stepping into their territory."

Reese shakes her head, her red hair falling over her shoulders. "But we're at the clubhouse, you guys don't go anywhere but around Merrill Hill."

"He means business-wise, Princess," I say, watching Allie while she stares at the cheap carpet.

Reese bites her lip, looking between Cale and me. "Oh," she pauses. "Are you?"

Callum shakes his head. "No, babe. We don't want anything to do with the shit that they're into." He lifts her hand to his lips, kissing the back. "Come on, Red, let's go home."

Reese nods and turns to Allie. "Are you okay?" She tries to ask quietly, but I hear her, and my spine straightens. What happened? Allie nods and releases Reese's hand, but Reese pulls her into a hug before standing and hugging me. "Talk to her," she whispers to me before pulling away and tucking under Cale's arm.

I follow behind them and close the door as they step into the hall. Turning around, Allie is still on my bed, staring at the floor. My heart sinks.

Walking to the bed, I sit beside her. "Talk to me, Al. What's going on?"

Allie finally looks up at me, and I wish she didn't. The tears in her eyes are breaking my heart worse than her refusing to look at me. "I slept with Saint again," she whispers.

My heart breaks a little. I turn to face forward, resting my elbows on my knees and leaning forward. Allie sits quietly at my side, but I feel her soft eyes on my back. I'm a little jealous, but I don't feel betrayed. I know how she feels about Saint, she has been honest about that since I found out about them. I know how he feels about her too, even if he does try to fight it.

"You love him, don't you?" I ask, no venom in my voice, but really it's not a question either; I already know what her answer is going to be, I just need to hear it from her. And I think she needs to hear herself admit it too.

"Yes," her voice cracks. "But I love you too.

I shake my head. "Don't do that, Al." I straighten up and turn to face her again. "I know how you feel about me, you don't have to protect my feelings when I ask you about him." She nods, a tear falling down her cheek, and I pull her into my chest where she collapses against me. "So you love Saint," I say softly into her hair.

"Yeah, and it breaks my heart every time he and I do this." She sniffles. "It breaks my heart that I did this to you," she cries.

I kiss her head, holding her to me tighter. "You didn't do anything, Solnyshko. I accepted a while ago that there was no us without Saint."

Allie pulls away, just enough so she can look up at me. "What?"

I lean into her and kiss her forehead. I hate that she's crying.

"He's a part of you, and no matter how much you love me, you won't be whole without him. Just like you wouldn't be whole without me." More tears fill her eyes and I pull her into my chest again. "Don't cry, Solnyshko. I know he'll come around, and I'm not ever leaving you." *No matter what happens*, I leave out.

32

ALLIE

The bell above the door dings as I step into the shop. Several mannequins with white dresses fill the front of the shop and my sandals sink into the plush, white carpet. A sales attendant greets me, and I smile politely as I point to the woman standing at the back, on the small pedestal, trying on her wedding gown.

Reese looks radiant in her dress. The low, v-cut neckline with the sheer fabric and lace flower applique covers the entire gown. It's perfectly Reese. Beautiful, sensual, and light. It'll look great on her and Callum's property. Their house isn't quite finished yet, but they set up a beautiful altar in the back that overlooks Mt. Rainier. They rented a nice restaurant in town for the reception. A quiet dinner with friends is all they wanted.

Reese's eyes catch mine in the mirror and she spins around. Her eyes are teary, but her smile is wide, and I step forward to hug her.

"Can you believe it?" she asks, pulling away and running her hands down the dress.

I shake my head, trying to hold back my own tears. "No," I laugh. "But also yes." I turn Reese around again so she's facing the mirror, and I watch her through it. "You and Callum are perfect together, but I never imagined that night at Mickey's would change our lives so drastically. That night seems like another lifetime ago."

She nods, adjusting the thin strap on her shoulder. "I agree, but I couldn't imagine a more perfect life for myself."

Another attendant steps out of a back room and I step back to sit in one of the light pink, velvet chairs behind Reese. I watch the attendant, who is actually the seamstress, point out all of the alterations she made on the dress. She turns Reese and lifts fabric—looking for any other changes that might need to be made—but there are none, because Reese looks perfect. Seeing Reese so happy with Cale has been everything I ever wanted for her, and I know she feels the same. I'm also a little selfish too, because if it hadn't been for Reese, I wouldn't have met Mason.

When the seamstress and Reese are satisfied with her dress, she brings out a bottle of champagne and two glasses, handing one to Reese and me and filling them before us. I stand and step over to Reese. "Cheers, babe. I can't wait to stand next to you tomorrow and watch you marry the man of your dreams. You deserve all of the happiness in the world, and I can't wait to watch Cale give it to you. I wish you so many years of love and comfort, and I know you'll get them. To forever."

"To forever. For both of us," Reese says, lifting her glass.

Rolling my eyes, I take a drink and set the glass down on the table next to me. We stare into the mirror and admire her and the dress. "I love you, babe." I take her free hand and squeeze it.

"I love you too, Al." Reese smiles at me. "Ah. Okay, I should get out of this before I spill champagne on it."

I take Reese's glass and help her down the step, following her to the dressing room where I stand beside the door, leaning against the wall and talking over the door to her. "Oh my God, I can't wait for all of the desserts at your wedding!" I groan. Reese has the biggest sweet tooth, so I know it's going to be over-flowing with sugar!

Reese chuckles, her throaty laugh floating over the door. "Me either." She pauses, and I can practically hear the hesitation in her voice. "Are you going with anyone tomorrow?"

"Yeah." I rest my head against the wall and down the rest of Reese's champagne. "Mason."

"So everything was good last night?" I hear a zipper on the other side of the door and more rustling.

"Yeah," I sigh. "Reese, he's perfect. Understanding, consider-ate. I can't help myself from feeling like he's wasting it on me."

Reese opens the changing room door and steps out carrying her dress bag. "Allie, Mason is head over heels for you, why would you think that?"

"Because Mason would do anything for me if I asked, but I still love a selfish, egotistical asshole. Or maybe I'm the selfish one, but I cannot choose between them. They make up both sides of my heart." I stare at the floor. I hate admitting this, even to my best friend.

She bumps my shoulder with hers, and I pick up my eyes to look at her. There's no judgment or anger there, only her beauti-ful, caring, green eyes. "Then why don't you go show Mason how much you love him, and let Saint come to you when he's ready?"

"What if he never does?" I ask quietly.

Reese shrugs. "I don't know, but I know you'll always have Mason. Would that be enough?"

I run my tongue over my bottom lip and think about that. "Yeah," I admit. "If Saint never spoke to me again, I would still have someone who I love, and someone who loves me. Mason would be enough, just like Saint would be enough if I didn't have Mason. I'd still be missing a part of me, though."

Reese nods and takes my hand. "Then come on, I know Mason's favorite burger place."

33

MASON

"Ugh!" I groan, leaning back in my chair and rubbing my eyes with my fingers. I send all of the files that Miles sent over from Ronan's phone to Saint, so he doesn't think I'm completely inept and can't do the one job I have for the club. I can't have him questioning me right now with everything going on. Things are already tense between us.

My door swings open and Allie steps through, smiling wide.

"Hey, beautiful. You were gone when I woke up," I say, watching her walk toward me. She's always beautiful, but today she looks like she's glowing. Her smile is bright, and her red lips are smiling back at me. Her silk, black dress brushes against her tan thighs, the top drooping a little and showing her cleavage. When my eyes get back to her face, her smile has turned into a smirk.

"I had to meet Reese for her final dress fitting." She steps past me and grabs some clothes from the dresser, taking them into the bathroom. "Get dressed, we're going out!" She closes the door before I can say anything, but based on the denim she grabbed, we must not be going anywhere that requires a dress code.

I dress in a white tee shirt, cut, and jeans, and grab a pair of Nikes. And when Allie steps out of the bathroom in one of my white tee shirts and denim shorts, I bark out a laugh.

She looks at me and then down at herself and laughs with me, bending over with her arms holding her stomach. She stands and grabs my hand, pulling me out of the room. "Come on, we're going to be late." I barely have time to grab my black hoodie off of my bed and my phone and wallet from my desk as I'm hauled out of my room.

"Where are we going?" I ask, watching her ass as we walk down the hallway. Sorry, I can't help it. She's perfect.

"It's a surprise, but you're driving. I want to take your bike." Music to my ears. Allie sitting as close to me as she can get, with her arms wrapped around me and holding me close. Hell yeah.

"How am I supposed to drive us somewhere if I don't know where we're going?" I pull her backward and under my arm as we get down to the main level of the clubhouse.

Allie holds out her hand, palm up. "Give me your phone, I'll put the address in and you can follow the directions."

I'd follow this girl to hell and happily stay by her side the entire time, so I hand her my phone. "Alright, Solnyshko, I'll bite."

She types as we walk out of the clubhouse and to my bike, her staying tucked into my body the whole way. The evening is warm with a light breeze. It's a great day for a ride with my girl.

When we get to the bike, I offer her my hoodie and she takes it, pulling it over her head and then pulling her hair into a ponytail.

"Wait, I'll do it," I say, turning her around so her back is to me and I can pull her hair back. When I'm done, I tie it off with the hair tie she offers me, and I put the helmet on her. The one I ordered for her after she rode on my bike the first time after Saint's promotion party.

She runs her hand down her braid and turns to me. "You braided my hair?" she asks, her eyes wide.

Shrugging one shoulder, I stare into her mint eyes, so unique and so her. Beautiful and soft. "I watched Reese do it a few times when she rode with me, but this was the first time I ever did it." I pick the end of the braid up over her shoulder and eye it again. It's not as good as Reese does, but it's alright.

Allie bites her lip to hold in her smile and fails, but I kiss her cheek and get on the bike, holding it up for her to get on too.

I don't recognize the address that Allie put into my maps app, but I follow it regardless, taking the drive slowly. She said she wanted to take the bike, so I assume she wants to enjoy the ride.

We're in Orca Bay, driving along the Sound. Allie taps on my shoulder and leans into my ear, "Can you turn up the radio? I love this song!"

"Roses" by GASHI plays from my bike stereo. My phone is hooked to it on Bluetooth. I turn the volume up and slow the bike down even more so we can hear it over the roar of the bike. I feel her helmet rest on my shoulders as she looks out over the water. The road is clear and the sun is getting low in the sky, and colors burst above us and over the water. This is the shit that's in movies, not in real life, but goddamn, my life feels like a movie right now. The perfect girl behind me, the perfect view, my bike, and I have the best friends I could ever ask for. My life is perfect right now.

This is everything I've ever wanted.

"Look!" Allie squeals, pointing out to the water. I turn my head just in time to see an Orca fin go under the water, and two more peak the surface before going back under.

Dropping my hand, I squeeze the hand that Allie has holding onto my shirt. I love this moment with her.

The GPS takes us to a park that backs up to the Sound. The

grass turns to sand that leads to the water. I park in the lot beside the park and help Allie off of the bike. We leave our helmets, and she pulls me along the sidewalk toward the park.

We walk by the playground equipment and keep going. The trees get a little thicker, and then the sidewalk ends, and we walk up a small, grassy hill.

At the top, I see a smiling redhead standing next to a blanket that's laid out across the grass.

"What are you doing here, Princess? You got a crush on me too?" I call to her, smiling.

Allie punches me in the side, though it was pretty weak, and Reese barks out a laugh.

"In your dreams, Underwood. If I was going to confess my love for anyone other than Cale, it would be Allie." Reese rolls her eyes.

I pull Allie in front of me and wrap my arms around her chest, hugging her to me. "Nope. I'm not sharing, Princess," I say, and Allie laughs loudly below me.

Reese shakes her head and starts to walk toward us. "I was just the one in charge of setting up while she brought you here. Have a good time tonight, you two, and don't be late tomorrow!" she yells as she walks past us.

Allie pulls out of my arms and walks over to the blanket. Without hesitation, I follow her, falling onto the blanket beside her.

Allie starts pulling out bag after bag, box after box. All from my favorite food places. The best mozzarella sticks from Kait's bar in the District. Burgers from the drive-in Reese and I go to, and tacos from my friend's taco truck that I took Allie to. Reese's brownies with frosting that she bakes and I love, and from a small cooler, Allie pulls out my favorite specialty beer that you can only get from one liquor store in town.

"How did you know?" I ask, looking over everything again. I can't believe she did this.

Allie smiles shyly, looking down at her hands as she arranges the food between us. "Reese helped a lot. We spent the afternoon baking and running around town to get everything. I haven't had as much time to get to know you yet."

I lean into her and kiss her. Pulling away, I say, "You will, Solnyshko. We both will."

Allie leans against me while we eat, and we watch the water, pointing out pods of orcas and watching the seagulls that sit a few feet away.

The sun starts to set, and I pack away all of our trash, picking it up and taking it to the trash can. When I come back, Allie is standing, holding her hand out to me.

"There's more?" I ask, my eyebrows shooting up.

"One more thing, I promise." She smiles.

I take her hand and she leads me down the hill and to the sand, where the water gently laps at the shore. No waves or anything, just gentle ripples in the water.

Allie lifts a small Bluetooth speaker that I didn't realize she had brought. I chuckle at the sight of it. "Do you want to dance with me, beautiful? I thought you were done with my antics after the last time at the taco truck."

Allie rolls her eyes. "Well, there isn't anyone here to watch us this time." She hands the speaker to me. "Just connect your phone and dance with me, Mase."

"Yes, ma'am." I smirk, taking the speaker from her and connecting my phone.

I play the song she said she liked during our drive, and my chest expands at the smile that crosses her face when the first chords of the song play.

Taking her in my arms, I hold her close as we sway to the music. The speaker sits in the sand, playing the song softly, and I rest my cheek on Allie's head that's resting against my chest. She watches the Sound, and I do too. Content with her in my arms.

That's what I feel. Perfectly content for the first time in my life. I have everything that I could ever want right here, right now.

I wish I could live in this moment forever.

When the song ends, Allie pulls away, leaning her head back to look at me. "Let's go back up and watch the sunset while we eat the brownies."

I nod and she pulls me up the little incline back toward our blanket. Allie curls up in my lap, laying her head on my thigh and looking up at me while I lean back on my arms and we talk about her courses for next year. Her summer break ends in about a month.

After the sun has set, Allie starts packing up our stuff and I watch her move around the blanket, clearing up the last of our stuff.

Taking her hand, I pull her toward me, directing her over my lap. I run my hand under her top, my hands sliding up her bare back, making her shiver.

"What are you doing?" she asks, her breathing getting heavier as my hands glide around the front of her body.

"I think it's obvious, Al," I whisper above her lips, leaning in to press a quick kiss.

Allie groans when I pull away, and I pull the cup of her bra away, my thumb circling over her nipple. "We're out in the open." She looks around.

"No one's here, and if you're quiet, no one will know." I look at her, pulling my hand away from her breasts. But she quickly holds my wrist still, not letting me pull my hand out of her shirt. Smirking, I know she's game for this. "No one's ever done anything like this for me. This picnic was the most heartfelt thing. I want to thank you."

I lift her off of me and place her on the blanket, following her body down so I'm settled between her legs. I slide down her body until I'm staring at the button to her shorts. She watches me while I undo it and slide her shorts and panties down her legs, setting them next to her on the blanket.

She shivers as a breeze passes over us, and I grin at her. She's so beautiful. Her blonde hair falls over her shoulder as she raises herself up on her elbows to watch me. Her mint eyes stare at me with the moonlight reflecting off of them. Her sun-kissed skin glitters when the light hits her. She looks like she stepped out of one of my dreams, and I want to take a picture of her and keep her like this forever.

Perfect. Mine. And wanting me.

She gasps when my breath ghosts over her sensitive skin, and I smile to myself before placing kisses on the inside of her thigh and then making a trail up to her clit. I use my hands to open her thighs more, spreading her open before me and staring at her. "What a beautiful little pussy." I use my tongue on her clit, flicking it side to side and then running my tongue along it, repeating the motions and listening to Allie's moans increase and get louder. "Shhhh, Solnyshko. You're going to get us arrested."

"Good thing I'm a law student," she groans and grinds her pussy into my face. Her small hands come down to weave into my hair and hold me where she wants me. I chuckle against her skin and the vibrations make her hips rise and she pulls on my hair harder. The stinging on my scalp only intensifies my arousal, and I dive into her.

Allie rocks her hips, riding my tongue as I press it against her clit, hard. She uses me how she wants, climbing higher and higher. One hand leaves her thigh to trail along her slit, feeling all of the wetness that has seeped out of her.

Fucking perfect. I slide two fingers into her easily, and she moans quietly, her hips picking up speed. I match my fingers to her pace, and I feel her pussy flutter over my fingers. I curl my fingers, feeling that spongy patch of skin on the inside, and massage that. She bursts.

Allie moans loudly before she slams her arm over her mouth and bites down on her skin. Fuck, she's amazing when she cums. Her pussy squeezes my fingers, and I wait until she's done before pulling out and rising up, sliding my jeans down my legs until they sit above my knees.

"My turn, Solnyshko," I growl, lining up my cock and sliding inside of her. It registers for a second that I didn't use a condom, but I ignore that the minute my balls slap against her skin, and all else is forgotten. I'm not going to waste any time though, her pussy squeezing my fingers made my cock jealous, and now I need to feel her pulsing around me.

I set a punishing pace, knowing that we're pushing our luck being out here—and although she's trying—Allie's not exactly quiet.

"You're so wet, beautiful. Do you like the idea of being caught?" I lean down and ask next to her ear. She whimpers and I know this is turning her on. The danger, anticipation, the thrill. "What about being watched? Do you want someone to watch me make you cum?"

"Mason," Allie moans and I almost blow my load then. I take a deep breath to calm myself.

"Do you want someone to watch how well you take my cock? To watch me split you apart and stretch you?" I continue. Allie pulls my mouth to hers, but when I kiss her she moans into my mouth loudly. "Do you want Saint to watch us?" I ask, my voice quieter than before.

"Oh God, I'm going to cum," she moans, but she's too late.

Her pussy starts to spasm around my cock and that's the last straw for me too. I cum with her, hot ropes shooting deep inside of her. Painting her as mine and claiming her.

Owning her.

She's mine, and although I might share her with another man, she will never belong to anyone but us.

34

ALLIE

Strong arms wrap around my stomach and pull me into a warm, hard chest, waking me.

"Good morning, Solnyshko," Mason says into my ear, his breath fanning against the lobe.

"Is it time to get up already?" I groan, squeezing my eyes shut. I don't want to get out of bed. It's warm and Mason is holding me like he thinks I'll run away if he loosens his hold.

He chuckles, laying his head back on the pillow. "Unfortunately, yes. Reese hasn't called yet, but I think we're living on borrowed time."

Rolling over, I stare into his beautiful sea-green eyes. "Will you drive me?"

Mason gives me a deadpan look. "Like I'm letting you out of my sight right now."

"You let me go to the bridal shop alone yesterday." I raise one brow in challenge.

He shakes his head. "I tracked your cell the entire day and checked in on surveillance videos when I could." My mouth drops and Mason laughs at me. I forget every day exactly what

Mason can do. "Get up and go shower, I'll order you a coffee that we can pick up on the way."

"No bike today, I don't want my hair to be wild and I need to take my dress," I say, reluctantly getting out of bed.

Mason chuckles, rolling onto his back and grabbing his phone. The sheet rests around his waist, and his tanned torso is on display. "I know, Solnyshko," he says. My steps falter and I contemplate climbing back in bed. Mason moves one arm up behind his head, his muscles bulging with the stretch, and his eyes peek over the top of his phone to watch my pause. "Do you want to get dirty before your shower, beautiful?" Mason sets his phone on the bed next to him and slides his hand under the sheet. I watch the movement of his hand, knowing that he's pumping himself. "Come on, Allie. Come be dirty with me." I take one look at the bathroom, and then back at Mason. He's biting his bottom lip and staring at me like I'm his breakfast, and I grab the bottom of his tee shirt and pull it over my head, dropping it on the floor and climbing over him on the bed.

THREE HOURS LATER, I step out of the bathroom at Soph's salon in my Maid of Honor dress. My hair and makeup are done, and Emma, Huntley, and Sophie are sitting in chairs sipping champagne, waiting for their turn to change, while an artist finishes Reese's makeup.

Once we're all dressed and ready to go, Nox and Wyatt will drive us to Reese and Callum's property and we're going to get our girl married. Reese's mom is in a chair next to her, barely holding in tears, as Reese scolds her to keep it together. Reese is barely keeping it together.

Reese notices me when I gesture to the other girls that I'm done in the bathroom and they can change. "Al! Oh my God, you look perfect!" The makeup artist finishes powdering Reese and steps aside.

"Thanks, babe. Are you doing okay? Can I get you anything? Champagne, water?" I ask, walking to her.

"No, I'm great. I'm just so excited to see him." Reese chokes on her words, and her teary green eyes look to the ceiling and blink rapidly.

I grab a tissue for her just in case she can't keep the tears at bay. "You look so beautiful." I pull a piece of her long curled hair over her shoulder. "He's going to lose his mind when he sees you."

Mrs. Thomas starts to sniffle, so she stands and walks away, leaving just me standing in front of Reese's chair. "I never thought this level of happiness was real. My life feels like a fairytale."

I take her hand, squeezing it and smiling at her. "I'm so happy for you. This is all I ever wanted for you. I love you, babe."

Reese squeezes my hand back. "I love you too, Al."

I take the tissue that I was supposed to give to her and wipe at my own eyes. "Oh my God! Okay." I compose myself. "Let's get you in your dress and get out of here. I'm hungry!"

Reese laughs and nods. I help her stand and after hugging Emma and Sophie one last time, Reese's mom and I step into the bathroom to help her get into her dress.

The property is beautiful. The house is half-built, but at least they have the siding up so it actually looks like a house. Not that it *really* matters, we're not doing anything with the house today, it would just be an eyesore.

A wooden altar stands close to the edge of the cliff. The wooden beams are thick, and a cream, gauzy fabric is draped over the top. The sun is starting to set, shining off of Mt. Rainier and making it reflect the colors back onto us.

This is perfect.

Chairs face the altar, and Callum stands tall in his white tux, with Jack standing next to him. I guess since he got ordained for Finn and Huntley's wedding, he does all of the club weddings now.

All of the wedding party are standing around the front of the house. We're lined up separately, waiting for our turns to go. Mason and Saint stand across from me. Mason smiles at me, he's always so bright and warm like the sun, and Saint does everything he can not to look at me at all. I shift in my wedges, uncomfortable being in front of them both at the same time after what happened the other night in the bathroom, but at the same time, my heart feels whole for the first time. I don't feel like I'm being pulled one way. I almost feel content. I just wish there wasn't so much anger between Saint and me. But I don't know what I could do to fix it other than leave Mason, and that's not an option.

Finn steps out first, walking down the aisle by himself and standing next to Cale as his best man. Saint is next, and before he walks around the side of the house, he looks at me. I'd like to say that regret is shining in his eyes, but I doubt he even knows the feeling. There's a pause in the procession between Saint and Mason because it's where Ronan should be. The music stops and everyone stands, and complete silence falls over the wedding. After a moment, the music starts again and that's Mason's cue to walk. As he passes me, he grabs my hand and kisses it, and then makes his way around the house.

It's my turn. I turn around to Reese and give her a hug. "I'll see you down there," I say next to her ear.

"What if I trip?" she laughs, but I can tell there are some tears behind it.

I pull away and look into her glittering green eyes. "Then I'll catch you." She nods and I release her, turning to walk down the aisle.

My stomach erupts into a fit of butterflies when I step around the house and see the aisle. People are sitting again, turned to watch everyone walk down, but all I see is Saint and Mason standing at the end. For a moment it feels like this is my wedding, and I let myself pretend that they are both waiting for me at the end. Mason's eyes are wide and his mouth is open as he stares at me. I hope he's imagining the same thing that I am.

Saint is guarded, as usual, but he's openly staring at me and not trying to hide it or look away, so I'd say that's progress. I switch my gaze between the two of them because I don't want to lose a second of this.

Emma, Sophie, and Huntley make their way down, but I don't take my eyes off of Saint and Mason, not until the music switches and I know Reese and Mr. Thomas are about to walk down.

Reese looks ethereal in her white gown with the sunset spilling over her. She looks like a garden fairy with her red hair hanging in loose curls down her back, the flower appliques on her dress, and the lush, green grass covering the ground. Her dad keeps his head up as he holds her hand on his arm. Reese is an only child, and she's very close to her parents, so I can imagine they're very emotional today. But when I look over at Callum, my heart swells for my best friend.

One tear slides down his cheek as he stares at Reese. I don't even think he blinks as she floats down the aisle to him.

I can't take my eyes off of her as she chuckles sweetly at Callum. Their love is a tangible feeling in the air, and looking out over the guests, they can all feel it too.

Reese and Mr. Thomas make it to the end of the aisle, and he passes her hand to Cale as she hands me her bouquet. "I'm trusting you with my baby," he says, his voice strong, though his eyes are glassy as he looks at Callum.

"I'll protect her with my life and love her until the day I die." Callum takes Reese's hand.

Mr. Thomas nods. "I know you will." He gives Callum a strong hug, patting his back before going to sit in the front row next to Mrs. Thomas, who holds a tissue up to her eyes and watches them.

I feel a pang in my heart watching Reese's dad with her. I wish my dad would be like that on my wedding day; that he would care about more than what my union could mean to him, and that he cared about my happiness more than his own gain. I remember that he gave me away to a man I've never met, a man who is the crime boss of the Russian mafia. He gave me away like an object, or maybe he sold me like I was cattle. I don't know for sure, and I don't care to. Both options are just as devastating. Maybe that's why I never formed attachments to men before or people in general. Reese, Sophie, and Emma were my first *real* friendships. Ones that were not formed just because we were in the same classes or because our parents wanted us to be friends for the connections. Mason and Saint were the first men I've ever felt this strongly for. I guess growing up with a father that would rather jet set the world for his career than be home with his only daughter, and a mother that chose another man over her family, taught me that I only needed myself. I like this version of my life better. I like having friends that would drop anything for me if I needed them, and I love having men who would fight for me and adore me. At least Mason adores me. Saint would fight for me, and with me, but at least he's there. And I would do all of that and more for them. I would go to the ends of the earth for Reese. I would destroy anything that hurt her. I would do that for all of my girls.

And Saint and Mason? There isn't anything I wouldn't do for them. Other than giving one of them up. I realize that I was staring off at the ground and quickly pick my head up. I meet

Saint and Mason's eyes when I do, mixed emotions written in both of them, so I minutely shake my head so they'll know I'm fine, even if Saint wouldn't care.

I tune back into the ceremony right in time for the vows. The sun is setting, and everyone is washed in a beautiful orange glow. We timed it perfectly; Mt. Rainier looks like it's glowing.

"Reese, you make my days brighter. You crashed your way into my life and brought it a new meaning. Every day I wake up the happiest man alive, and I can't wait to come home to you after work. I can't wait to spend the rest of my life eating your burnt food," Cale stops his speech to laugh when Reese swats his arm. Everyone laughs with him, while Reese glares at him, trying to hold in her laughter. He continues, "And eating the amazing things you bake afterward to make up for it. I can't wait for our house to be done and to be able to see this same sunset for the rest of our lives. Every day we'll look out of the window and see the place where we vowed to love each other forever, and I can't think of anything better than that." He takes a deep breath and stares at Reese for a moment. "I love you more than anything I've ever known, and I promise to make any dream you have come true. Forever, Red."

"Callum," Reese starts. "I had given up on love when you found me. But slowly and without my noticing, you made me fall in love with you. You showed me that love doesn't have to end in heartbreak, and through just being my friend, you helped me learn to love myself again. You swooped in and saved me on the night that we met, and you've been doing that every day since. You made my dream life come true, because my dream was you, even if I didn't know you yet. I love you today, tomorrow, and forever." Reese and Cale smile at each other and hold hands, their love blinding everyone, and I bring the tissue in my hand to my eyes to dab at the tears that threaten to fall. I'm overjoyed for my best friend. Mason catches my eye when I look up, hiding the tissue back in my hand that's wrapped around my small bouquet.

He smiles and mouths *I love you.* I open my mouth to say it back, but loud applause makes me snap my head to where Cale is dipping Reese and he's kissing her as her hands wrap tightly around his neck. Oops, I guess we missed the "I do's."

Finn whoops when Cale stands back up with Reese. They join hands and walk down the aisle, back to Cale's truck so they can take pictures while we all head to the restaurant.

After Cale and Reese make it down the aisle, Finn steps out and grabs Huntley's hand, leading her away. They're both too beautiful to be real, and they look even more unreal together. Jesus, their kids are going to be beautiful.

Saint is next in line on the men's side, and although I know he's not going to choose me to walk away with, it still hurts when he walks by me without even glancing at me. I stare at the ground and only look up when I see a tan hand reaching out for me.

Mason smiles down at me and I take his hand, letting him lead me around the front of the house and to the limo. I catch Saint's back as he speeds away on his bike. His cut is thrown over his cream dress shirt. Mason gets into the limo with me, Sophie, Emma, and Reese's parents. Callum's were, of course, absent. I doubt they even knew he was getting married today. Actually, I doubt they even know about Reese at all, and for that, I feel sorry for them. Sorry that they're missing out on their son's happiest day, missing out on meeting their daughter-in-law— the love of their son's life. But I don't feel sorry for Cale, if they would cut him off that easily, he deserved better anyway.

Maybe we could start a shitty parents club.

35

SAINT

ALLIE SITS TOWARD THE END OF THE LONG TABLE NEXT TO REESE, with Mason on Allie's other side. She looks reserved, keeping her head down and whispering to Mason, but keeping a slight distance between them. I wonder if she can feel me watching her? If she misses me? If she's mad about how the other night turned out?

I didn't mean to lose control and fuck her in the bathroom, and I didn't want to leave her afterward, but I was so confused about what just happened, and that I had just fucked a brother's girl. Are Allie and Mason dating, or are they doing what we were doing? I didn't want to push her away, but when I saw the Kings, I wasn't going to let any of them see her. I would gouge out their eyes before they got a chance.

Fuck. It's easier to be mad at her when I'm sober. When I'm drunk I just realize how much she hurt me and how I'm not over it, or over her.

Cale and Reese rented out the entire restaurant, so it's just the club, Reese's friends, her family, and Randy here. The lights were lowered in the restaurant so it feels more intimate, and the string lights brighten the wooden patio that sits over the Sound.

Nothing was spared, especially not the dessert table, covered with a giant wedding cake, donuts, cupcakes, and macarons. This place is overflowing with food and alcohol. Which is all I need.

I start drinking the moment I step into the restaurant, and I don't stop until Nox is pushing me into an Uber and following me in.

"What are you doing?" I slur, resting my head against the window.

He slams his door and gets comfortable in the seat next to me. "Making sure you get home all right."

My eyes close as I let the cool window rest against my warm forehead. "I don't need help, I could get home by myself."

He scoffs and I feel the car move forward. "I was not letting you try to ride, you are way too drunk."

I roll my eyes, even though they're closed. That's how stupid what he just said was, I had to roll my closed eyes. "I meant I could get my own cab. I didn't ask you to escort me home, Prospect."

"I'm not doing this because I'm a Prospect, I'm just trying to help a struggling brother," he says softer this time.

"I'm perfectly fine," I sigh.

Softly, almost whispering, he says, "No you're not, and she's not either."

Thankfully, Nox shuts up and leaves me to myself, but also not thankfully, my mind wanders when he does that. Back to the last wedding we attended together.

ONE MONTH AGO...

"Hey, are you leaving?" I hear Allie's sweet voice yell behind me, her heels clicking against the concrete as she hurries toward me.

Turning around, I watch her, wondering how she hasn't fallen and broken her ankle. Leave it to Allie to show up to a biker wedding in a designer dress and heels. I remember that I haven't answered her and am just staring at her when her eyes widen slightly. "Yeah, I have to go do something for the club." Go torture another spy is what I'm actually doing, but I probably shouldn't admit that to her.

"Could I convince you to take me home? I came with Reese and she's staying behind to help clean up, but I have a flight I have to catch." She shifts on her feet, her dress swaying with her. The black bustier top with the thick, fluffy skirt looks perfect on her.

I realize I'm staring again, and gesture to my Audi. "Yeah, I can take you." I've never been more glad that my bike was in the shop getting new tires. That much dress on the back of a bike would not have worked.

I open the door for her and offer my hand for her to hold as she slides into the car. "Thank you." She avoids my eyes with a small smile on her face and sits down in the Audi.

I get in myself and start the engine, admiring the purr before I pull out of the driveway and start down the long road back into Merrill Hill. "You have a late flight, is everything okay?" I ask, watching the road, but looking at Allie out of the side of my vision.

She sighs and locks her phone, placing it back into her clutch. "Yeah, my dad wants me to attend a business meeting with him tomorrow night. Stable family man and all that." She rolls her eyes. "I didn't want to go, but he made the reservation for my favorite restaurant, and I can spend all day tomorrow shopping, so I guess why not, right?"

She sounds like going to see her father is the last thing she wants to do. I doubt her dad is going to a legal meeting, though he's supposed to defend the law. I looked into him as I'd gotten to know little Allison Lenkov. Her father is bought by anyone with enough money. "Sounds fun."

Allie scoffs, looking out of the window. "Hardly."

"I can get myself arrested and insist that Mr. Johnson brings you

along to bail me out," I suggest. Allie looks at me with wide eyes again, so I continue. "If you want an excuse as to why you'll miss your flight tonight."

Allie opens her mouth, then closes it and purses her lips. Finally, she says, "You'd do that for me?"

The emotion sparkling in her beautiful eyes makes my heart stutter and my brain wakes the hell up. I shrug one shoulder, turning my focus back to the road. "I'm feeling generous tonight," I say to try and diminish my offer.

She hums in agreement. "Thank you, but I think the only excuse my father will accept is if I were the one arrested."

"I can make that happen too." I glance at her.

Allie bursts out in laughter. Loud, beautiful laughter that I'd never heard from her. "Let's not."

I dip my head to the side. "The offer is always there."

We drive the rest of the way in silence, and when we get to her house, she pauses with her hand on the door.

"Thank you, Saint," she says softly.

Before she gets out of my car and I lose this moment between us—because although there haven't been many, and they're always fleeting, they never leave my mind—I place my hand on her arm, stopping her. I lean over the center console slowly, allowing her time to back out if she wants, and when she leans toward me instead of running, I feel like my whole world starts to spin faster. Our lips meet in a slow, hesitant kiss, and it's over before I even get to taste her for real. She raises a hand to her mouth and gently touches her lip. I want to grab her by the throat and pull her back to me and bite that lip. When I don't say anything, she turns around and reaches for the door again.

"I'll be your Clyde, whenever you need me," I say when she opens the door. Allie giggles and nods, widening the door and getting out without another word.

I wait until she's unlocked her door and gotten inside before I drive *away, wishing that she wasn't about to fly across the country to go be with her slimy father, and instead was staying here with me so we could explore what we just started.*

There isn't a doubt that Allie will be mine, because she already is. She has been for a while now.

PRESENT...

I hear the locks click on the door and I open my eyes, seeing my house, and then I hear the door next to me open. I kind of forgot Nox was with me.

"Thanks, man!" Nox hollers as he slides out of the car.

I clear my throat and sit up, undoing my seatbelt. "Thank you," I say before I get out.

I pass Nox and walk to my front door. "Nice house," he says from behind me.

Unlocking the door, I walk inside and flip on the hall light. "You're sleeping on the couch. Don't wake me in the morning." He follows me inside, and I go straight to the kitchen, grabbing the bottle of vodka from the freezer and a bottle of water from the fridge. I leave the kitchen and exit the house to the backyard, sitting in one of the chairs down on the lawn that faces the water.

I lift the bottle and take a long swig, letting the vodka slide down my throat. My phone vibrates in my pocket, so I set the bottle on the grass to pull my phone out.

UNKNOWN:

We can meet tomorrow in New York. I'll send
you a time and place tomorrow.

New York? It has to be Mikhail.

SAINT:

I thought we were speaking through Miles, how
did you get my number?

MIKHAIL:

That's a really useless thing to ask me.
Tomorrow or not at all.

I exhale loudly and set my phone on the wide arm of the chair, picking up the bottle to take another big drink.

Fuck. This really could be it for me.

Before I really even think about what I'm doing, I pick my phone back up and hit call on Allie's number.

It rings out to the voicemail, without her answering, and I should hang up. This is a sign that I shouldn't have called her, but I can't get myself to hang up.

"This is Allie, leave a message," her sweet voice says down the line.

Beep. The loud tone echoes through my head. "I don't even know why I'm doing this," I start. "I guess because this might be the last time I ever get to say anything to you. Do you remember Finn and Huntley's wedding? The night that I drove you home and kissed you for the first time? I wish I wouldn't have let you go that night. Maybe everything would have been different. You would have gotten to know me before everything went to shit. Before Ronan." I clear my throat, not letting myself cry anymore. "I pictured us up there today. When I saw you standing by the altar, I pictured us standing in front of our friends and vowing to love each other for the rest of our lives." I pause, anger taking over me again, just like it did during the ceremony. "And then I remembered you're fucking someone else and I wanted to die." Taking another drink, I let the liquor smooth out the edges of my rage. "Maybe tomorrow will be better. I won't be here to make myself suffer anymore, to make you suffer." The water ripples under the moonlight and the silence of the world sets in around me. I've made peace with this. I know what I have to do, but first Allie needs to know this. "I love you, Allie. And I hate you. I wanted you to choose me, but you chose him. Regardless of everything though, I just want you to be happy, even if it kills me." I pull the phone away from my ear and hang up. That was already too much, too deep. I kill the rest of the bottle of vodka and take it and the water bottle back to the house. I'll down the water and head to bed. I have places to be tomorrow.

36

ALLIE

SAINT'S VOICE PLAYS THROUGH MY PHONE AND I QUICKLY PULL IT away from my ear to rewind the voicemail and play it again. Mason walks into his bedroom while I'm focusing on the comforter and listening to Saint tell me... I don't even know what he's trying to tell me. He's clearly drunk, slurring most of his words, but I can understand him perfectly. This feels like a goodbye.

Mason sets my coffee on the bedside table, falling onto the bed at my feet. I'm sitting in the bed, my back rod straight and my knees brought up to my chest. When I woke up this morning and saw the voicemail, I expected scathing words and I figured I could hug myself while I cried, but instead, panic seeps into my bones. This doesn't feel right.

"What's going on?" Mason asks, studying my face.

I pull the phone away and play the voicemail for him, and I watch him while he listens, looking for a clue somewhere on his face. He chews his lip while he stares at my phone, listening to Saint. "What does he mean he won't be here?" I ask. Mason looks up at me and shakes his head. Letting out a sigh, I dial Saint's number and wait for him to answer. He doesn't. So I try again. And again. After the fourth call that goes unanswered, the panic fully sets in and my hands start to shake. "We need to find him," I say, but Mase is already standing and walking to his computer.

I follow him and rest my hands on his shoulders as he pulls up a big map and types in Saint's phone number. The map zooms out to show the globe and the globe spins a few times before it quickly zooms in and shows what I'm pretty sure is Saint's house. There's an address in the top corner, but the map is from the top view and I don't know Saint's address. "He's at his house."

"Take me please, Mase," I beg, my hands squeezing his shoulders.

He stands hurriedly. "Yeah, but put on some pants first." He looks down at my bare legs.

Right. I rush to his dresser and pull a pair of jean shorts out of my temporary drawer. No offense to Mason, but I can't wait to go home. He can come with me, but I will be so glad to have more than a few drawers.

The drive to Saint's house feels like it takes forever. I stare straight ahead the entire time, looking over Mase's shoulder. I don't even watch the water as we speed by on his bike. It's so different going down this road this time than the other two times I came down it with Saint and then with Mason.

Mase pulls into the driveway and I hop off of the bike and run to the door before Mason has the chance to put the kickstand down or shut off the bike. I bang on the door, slamming my fist into it as hard as I can and yelling Saint's name.

Mason joins me and pounds his fist against the door as well. We probably bang on the door for five minutes before it finally opens, but it's not Saint.

Nox opens the door, rubbing his eyes and squinting at us.

"Where's Saint?" I yell, pushing him aside and storming into the house.

I hear the door shut behind me as I stalk through the house to check the kitchen and living room for him. "Upstairs sleeping, Jesus. What's going on?"

I turn and run up the stairs, taking the steps two at a time. Feet pound on the stairs, so someone is following me, but I don't turn around to check who.

I remember the route to Saint's bedroom and I don't waste any time slamming the door open and walking in, but I stop in my tracks when I see what a disaster his room is.

Broken furniture is thrown everywhere. The dresser is away from the wall and has a huge hole in it, the bed is in several pieces, and the lamps are broken and scattered on the floor. What the fuck happened in here?

I step through the room carefully and walk to the bathroom, sucking in a breath when I see the mural drawn on the mirror.

Walking to it hesitantly, I feel my heart break in my chest. There's a picture of me, drawn in what looks like red lipstick or something. I'm sleeping, and I can only assume it's from the morning after I stayed the night. There's glass scattered across the bathroom vanity, pieces of a lamp and half of the shattered mirror laying there.

Saint did this. He did all of it.

"I'm going to check the rest of the house," Mason says gently behind me, and I nod, not taking my eyes off the drawing. After taking a minute to breathe and take in the mural, I leave his room. Saint is obviously not in here, so I meet Mason in the hallway and he shakes his head. "He's not up here, but he has been sleeping in one of the spare rooms. I found his phone." He holds up his phone to show me.

We run back down the stairs and I go to the back door while Mason goes somewhere else in the house.

I search the entire backyard and around the outside of the house, but he isn't anywhere out here. I was kind of hoping he might have passed out, out here, last night after calling me. Walking back inside, I find Mason and Nox standing by the kitchen island. "His Audi is gone."

"Our bikes should still be at the restaurant. I came back here with him in an Uber," Nox says, pulling the shirt he was wearing last night over his head.

"Okay, let's go check the restaurant before we freak out." Mason stares directly at me, and I nod, stepping around them to leave the house.

Mason helps me back onto his bike and Nox steps up beside us. "I'll call Leo to take me to the restaurant and then I'll go back to the clubhouse. Call me if you need anything or when you find him."

Mase nods and pulls us around and out of the driveway.

My knees start to bounce on the footpegs. I have a terrible feeling. Mason's hand drops to one of my legs and he squeezes just above my knee. The warmth of his hands calms me a bit, and I hug him tighter and take a deep breath of his scent. I'm still wearing his tee shirt that I slept in last night.

Saint and Nox's bikes are still parked in the restaurant parking lot, and since they don't serve breakfast, they're still closed.

The lot is empty except for the two bikes.

"Mason," I whine. "I'm about to lose it."

He runs his hands through his hair, pacing back and forth by the bikes. "I know, Al. Let me make a few calls, okay? I think I might know where he went." He pulls his phone out of his pocket and curses under his breath. That doesn't make me feel any better. He dials a number and places the phone to his ear. "Hey, are you with Saint?" He tries to turn his back to me, but I step around him, not letting him turn away from me. "He left

Allie a weird voicemail last night and now we can't find him." He pauses and rolls his eyes. "Yes, it said he was at his house so we went there, but he left his phone behind and took his Audi somewhere." Mason sighs heavily. "Can you just trust that when I say we can't find him that we looked everywhere for him? He's not at the restaurant. His bike is still here." Mason looks at me briefly before looking away again. "Did you hear anything about that meeting?" What meeting? "Okay, yeah. Call his shop and I'll call Miles." Mason hangs up but doesn't look at me, just focuses on his phone.

"What meeting, Mason?" I ask carefully.

He licks his lips, looking nervous. "Just let me talk to Miles and I'll tell you everything okay? I promise, just give me a minute." I nod and he focuses back on what he's doing. "Hey, have you heard from Mikhail about that meeting?" No. No, no, no. Not Mikhail. "Fuck," Mason breathes. "I think Saint went to meet him by himself. He was supposed to take Finn, but he hasn't heard from him since last night at the wedding."

37

SAINT

KNOCK, KNOCK. I ROLL OFF OF MY HOTEL BED AND WALK TO THE door, checking the peephole before opening it for the attendant with my room service.

"Hey thanks, man. Here." I pass him a hundred-dollar bill to try to hurry him out of my room.

Luckily, he takes the cue and leaves me with my plates, exiting quickly. The small breakfast at the airport wasn't enough, and when I got to New York I didn't want to deal with getting food anywhere. I just wanted to eat and then nap until I got the text about the meeting. I bought a new burner cell when I got to New York and sent Mikhail my new number. I left my phone at home so no one could track me. Mason might track my Audi to the airport, and they'll probably know I came here, but that's all they'll know. I pulled out cash for the hotel so they couldn't find out where I'm staying.

They'll see me in Merrill Hill if I make it back home.

Food and a short nap make me feel a ton better, and I lounge around my hotel room, watching TV for a few hours before my cell finally pings with a text.

Typing the address into the maps app, I zoom out and see he

wants to meet me down at the harbor. Fuck, he really is going to kill me.

Shoving one gun into the inside pocket of my cut, I take a deep breath and leave my room. I have an hour to get there and I can't waste any time waiting around debating my decision. I already made it when I asked to meet with him and then left without telling anyone.

I refuse to think about Allie, because that shits just too hard to think about right now. The inner war I'm fighting to go back to Washington and steal her away, and knowing that I'm doing this for her. I try to distract myself on the ride down, but my thoughts keep circling to Ronan. Would he do the same thing that I am? How pissed I'd be that he left without me. I'd be on the next flight out and spend the entire day and night looking for him in New York. Not that, that would be the best thought-out plan, but I know that I'd panic and chase after him. I think he would do the same thing though, sacrifice himself for the club. Something clicks inside of my head, something big slotting into place. Is that why he was in that alley? Is that why he died? Was he saving us from something? I knew he wasn't mugged.

I pull out my phone and open a new text.

SAINT:

Did you know?

ACE:

Know what, Saint?

How does he fucking know everything? I just got this number this morning.

SAINT:

That Ro wasn't just mugged.

ACE:

Yes.

SAINT:

Were you ever going to fucking say anything
to me?

ACE:

No.

I'm going to kill him. If I walk away from this meeting, I'm finding his white-haired ass and killing him.

SAINT:

Why didn't you say anything? I would have
killed them. Who was it?

ACE:

I don't know. I just know that it was more than a
mugging. I can't get involved. If you need
anything else, I will hold up my offer of help, but
I cannot help you with this.

Dropping the phone, I drag my hand over my face. He was no fucking help and only made this more confusing.

The cab comes to a stop, and I look out at the lights of the harbor. Paying the driver, I step out and start to walk to the warehouse that Mikhail had sent me the address to. It's warm tonight, the moon is climbing the sky, and the city lights replace the stars.

The street is empty, and the only sign of life is my taxi that's quickly leaving, his taillights shining like a warning as they get smaller and smaller.

The warehouse is a large gray building with no lights or windows. It doesn't look like anything, and it takes me a while of walking down the sidewalk until I come across a metal door. Trying it, I pull it open and step inside.

Immediately, a hulk of a man is stopping me, staring me down. I open my arms for him to frisk me. "I'm here to meet Mikhail Belov. My name is Saint. Gun is in the inner pocket of my cut," I say, making eye contact with the guy.

He grunts, grabbing my gun and then my phone from my front pocket. "I know who you are." He feels me up, and when he's certain that I don't have any other weapons, he gestures to the stairs. "Upstairs."

Stepping around him, I go to the metal stairs and take them up. Upstairs is another wide open, empty space, but up here, there are large windows that overlook the water and the city lights from the other islands.

"Mr. Viotto. I'm afraid we've never met," Mikhail Belov's voice booms from in front of the windows. He slowly turns around. His gray tux fits perfectly to his large frame, and his goons stand around casually with ARs slung over their chests, watching me.

"We haven't," I answer, walking toward him confidently.

"Then why are you here? And alone." His brown eyes narrow on me as I get closer. He's built a lot like Finn, taller and much wider than me.

I clear my throat and stop a few paces away from him. "To talk about Vadim."

I hear feet shifting and when Mikhail holds up a hand to his men, I chance a glance around. Yup. They're all aiming at me. Cool. "Where is he?" Mikhail asks, seemingly calm, but his eyes flare.

I take a deep breath, but I don't make it noticeable. Looking to the side at one of the guys with the rifles again, I face Mikhail and lie because Allie's life depends on it. "I killed him." I feel a muzzle press against the back of my head, but I keep my spine straight and my eyes focused on Mikhail.

"It's rather brave of you to ask to meet with me and then tell me you killed my Brigadier." Mikhail crosses his arms over his wide chest and stares down at me.

"I didn't know who he was. He broke into my Old Lady's house and was trying to kidnap her. I didn't know why, I was just protecting my girl." He doesn't need to know the specifics.

"Allison Lenkov," he supplies.

I nod, as much as I can with the gun digging into my scalp. "I found out later that her father promised her to you, but she's not going anywhere. She's property of the Devil's Outlaws."

His eyes drop to my cut and he bites the side of his lip. "You're the President."

"I am, and I know you need justice for your man. That's why I'm here talking to you, but if you take me out or go after Allie again, you'll be taking on the entire organization." The gun at the back of my head presses a little harder, making my head push forward, but Mikhail waves him off and I feel the gun and the man retreat.

Mikhail wets his lips, light glinting off of his gold rings while he cracks his knuckles. "Tie him up," he says calmly.

A hood is thrown over my head and I'm knocked to the floor. I fight against them, but I have no idea how many guys land down on me and wrestle me until they get my hands behind my back and tie them together, then move on to my legs. I think I nail one guy in the balls because someone groans loudly, and then a hard kick in the ribs knocks the wind and the fight out of me. They drag me across the concrete floor by my tied arms and toss me against a wall, my head bouncing off of the concrete and sending stars fluttering across my closed eyes.

Well, fuck. I try to strain my ears to hear what's going on, but I only hear slight footsteps and shuffles as the guys move around the warehouse, most of them seem to be congregating around me.

After a little while, I hear the soft clacks of dress shoes against the floor and then the hood is being ripped from my head, and Mikhail is kneeling in front of me.

"Your story checks out." He glares at me.

"And you don't have the numbers to go against us," I say. Not arrogantly, just stating the facts. Internationally, they would decimate us, but here in the U.S.? Yeah, we got them beat big time.

"I'm out a wife and a closely trusted Brigadier and friend because of you, so what are you suggesting you do to compensate for that? If not your life, then who's?" he asks.

I shrug—kind of. "Whoever. Why did Alexei give you Allie?"

Mikhail rubs his hand across his thick, dark beard. "He lost a case and got a few of my men sent away. They were killed in prison."

A joy that is absolutely wrong settles in my gut. "Then I'll kill Alexei for you."

"He's my lawyer," Mikhail says, cocking his head and watching me.

I narrow my eyes. "It's New York City, I'm sure you can find another lawyer for sale."

"What about my wife?" Mikhail counters.

Baring my teeth, I say calmly. "Allie is off limits. I'll find you someone else if you're really that bad at finding your own women." The last part was half a joke.

He cocks one eyebrow. "You don't scare easily."

I look away briefly before meeting his eyes again, letting the truth shine through my eyes. "Nothing is more terrifying than losing the woman you love."

Mikhail nods once and then stands and steps away, gesturing

to me. A few of his men step forward and untie my legs and hands, and I stand up slowly, rubbing at my wrists.

"I want confirmation of Alexei's death. My men will take care of the body." Mikhail watches me.

I lick my lips, thinking over the consequences of this deal. It's worth it. "Okay, let me go home and talk to my club. It'll be done by the end of the week."

"That's exactly how long you have before I come to Washington and find your club," Mikhail says.

I take that as my cue to leave, and I confidently make my way out of the warehouse, retrieving my gun and phone from the guy still standing by the door.

Now I have to go home and tell Allie that I have to kill her dad, or I'm dead and she's got a new husband.

38

SAINT

I ALREADY KNOW MASON—AND MOST LIKELY—ALLIE ARE AT MY house as I pull into the garage, because his bike is sitting in my driveway. I'm slightly annoyed, but I know that I need to talk to them anyway, so I guess it's for the best. I just want to go to fucking sleep. My head was already fucked up when I woke up this morning with a wicked hangover, then goon number one bounces my head like a basketball off of a concrete wall, and it didn't get any better on the plane home. I'm tired, I'm hungry, and I don't want to deal with everyone. Also, I'm still pissed about the realization about Ronan and I need to figure out where that theory can lead us. Maybe we'll actually get some answers now.

I step into my house from the garage and hear low murmurings from the TV. "Can we please make this quick? I'm tired and hungry." Just as I say that, I notice a pizza box sitting on my counter, so I walk over and take a slice out and turn around to grab a water bottle from the fridge.

"Saint!" Allie gasps.

"Yeah, we're going to talk about your breaking and entering later." I turn around and lean over the pizza box to eat.

Allie runs to me, slamming into my chest so hard that I stagger backward while I wrap one arm around her. I shouldn't do this, I shouldn't let her in. but it feels too good, and she's probably going to hate me after I tell her what I have to do. I might as well enjoy this while I still can.

Mason comes in from the living room, hanging back from intervening or whatever. His arms are crossed and I know he wants to say something. "Go ahead, say it," I hedge. A fight would be the perfect distraction right now.

"Why did you go alone? We were so worried." Allie pulls away from me and leans her head back to look at me.

Chewing my bite, I think over how to answer her. I go with the truth. "Because I didn't know how this was going to end up, and I wasn't risking any of my brothers. That was the whole point in going to begin with."

"Finn's pretty pissed," Mason supplies.

I narrow my eyes at him. "He can be pissed. He's alive. I wasn't sure I was going to be for a bit there."

"What was the meeting about? What's going on?" Allie asks, pushing away from me and leaning against the counter. She looks upset. I guess we did kind of leave her in the dark a little bit.

I look at Mason again, seeing if he wanted to be the one to tell her, but I guess that should be me since I made the call. "I had to meet with Mikhail to tell him about Vadim, and that he couldn't have you." Allie's eyes widen, but I already know where she's going next. "He doesn't know about Mase, he needed to know what happened when he sent someone for you, that way he wouldn't send anyone else."

"What happened?" she whispers.

I look into her mint eyes, not sure if I'm going to destroy her entire world or if she'll even care. After Alexei sold her to someone she's never met, behind her back, I wouldn't assume she'd be his biggest fan, but I don't know what their relationship is like. "We made a deal," I finally say.

"Which is?" Mason asks, slowly walking into the kitchen with us.

"Mikhail wants revenge," I say slowly.

Allie's eyes widen and her face turns pale. "For Vadim?"

Taking another bite, I sway my head from side to side. "And for other things."

"Who?" Mason asks, standing tall—like I'd give his ass up or something.

"Your father." I look at Allie and watch probably a million different emotions pass over her face. She stays like that for a long time, staring off over my shoulder, her face a perfectly confused mask.

"But you both will be safe? And Mikhail will leave me alone?" she asks quietly, her head flicking between Mason and me.

"Yeah." I nod. "I think I also have to hook him up with another wife, but we can worry about that one later."

"Okay," she sighs. "Whatever will keep the three of us safe."

Mason finally closes the gap between us, clutching Allie's arm. "Al, are you sure? We can figure something else out."

"He sold me, Mason. Behind my back. To a criminal that I've never met before. I was almost kidnapped. Who knows what type of life I would have had if Vadim had succeeded. There was no promise that I would have been safe. He didn't care about me at all. He never has, only what I could do for him." She turns to me with the beautiful fire in her eyes that I've always loved. "Why did he do it anyway?"

"He let some of Mikhail's guys go to prison and they were killed there. He traded your life for theirs," I tell her plainly. There's no sense in sugar-coating it.

She shrugs, turning back to Mason. "Now it's his life for theirs, which is how it should have been in the first place."

39

SAINT

ALLIE SWEARS SHE'S FINE. OVER AND OVER, SHE REASSURED Mason and me, but that doesn't stop me from feeling a little bad about what I'm on my way to do. I sent Allie and Mason back to the clubhouse after they stayed for a while and we both obsessively watched over Allie, continuously asking her the same question. Now that we have Mikhail's agreement, she can move back into her house. I could tell that Allie didn't want to go, but I wasn't going to let them stay in my house with me. I might be letting go of my anger toward her a little bit, but it doesn't change the fact. She chose him.

"Thank you so much for allowing me to come this time," Finn snarks as he deftly lands in the seat across the aisle from me.

Rolling my eyes, I buckle my lap belt. "I bought you a first-class ticket, I think that's enough of an apology."

"Actually…" Finn trails off, looking at the entrance of the plane.

"I'm coming too!" Nox sits down next to me with a wide smile.

I narrow my eyes at him. "Why are you here?"

His smile is so wide that I think it might split his face. "I've never been to New York, I wanted to come."

Dragging my hand down my face, I groan. "You bought him a ticket too?" I gesture toward Nox.

Finn shrugs. "And some toys for Noctem, but don't worry, I'll tell her they're from Uncle Saint."

Shaking my head, I turn back forward. "I'm never trusting you with my card info again."

"Don't worry, I wrote it down." He smirks and I chuckle under my breath. "Oh, by the way, I finished the K-Model. Leo will have it waiting for you when we land back here tonight."

Nodding, I pull out my sketch pad and a pencil and distract myself the entire flight.

When we land, we take a cab back to the same hotel I stayed in a few days ago, and check into our rooms.

Not long after we settle into our rooms, there's a knock at my door, and I open it to let in Finn and Nox.

"So what's the plan, Prez?" Finn asks, sitting in the armchair that's against the wall.

I settle on the bed while Nox lounges on the bench seat at the window. "Alexei lives alone so I suggest we go to his house and do it there. Mikhail is taking care of the disposal, so we just have to get it done. I was thinking a simple break-in with a suppressor."

"What about security?" Finn leans back in the chair and widens his legs, getting comfortable.

"Just a simple door alarm that Allie gave me the code for. She was here a few months ago so she knows it's accurate," I say.

Nox stretches out on the bench. "When?"

I roll my shoulders, loosening up the muscles from the stressful past month I've had. "Tonight. Mikhail hasn't said anything about the failed mission to get Allie, so he has no idea."

Finn stands. "Alright, let's go get some food before then. I also have to find some souvenirs for Huntley, so let's go."

Shaking my head, I stand too. "Whipped," I quip.

"Hell yeah, I am!" Finn says proudly, walking to the door with Nox and me following him.

Hours later, mid-day has turned to night, and the neighborhood of the Lenkov brownstone is quiet.

Finn, Nox, and I creep down the sidewalk, walking quietly and watching our surroundings for anyone watching or anything that might be off. I take the four steps up to the door and step aside to let Finn pop the lock. He's in better practice and is quicker. He gets it done and pushes the door open, and I quickly step past him and enter the code before the alarm can sound. The lights are off downstairs, but the lights on the stairs are on. Finn starts wandering around the house, using his phone's flashlight. I head to the stairs and turn around when I notice Nox following me.

"Can I fucking help you?" I ask, glaring at him.

He takes a step back. "I was just going to look around upstairs."

Rolling my eyes, I go back to the stairs and quietly climb them to the second floor. Upstairs there are several doors, but only one has lights shining through the bottom of the closed door at the end of the hall. I turn left, towards the door, and Nox goes right.

I roll my feet as I walk so I don't create footsteps on the hardwood floors. Pressing my ear against the door, I can hear the shower running faintly, so I pop the door open slightly and peek in. No one is in the bedroom, so I step through and see light and steam billowing out from the ensuite bathroom. There isn't a door, just a wide doorway that leads to what looks like an expansive bathroom. I look around the room before taking a seat on the bench at the foot of the bed and wait for Alexei to come out.

I wait for about ten minutes when I hear the shower cut off. Alexei walks out with a towel wrapped around his waist. He jerks in surprise and his eyes widen when he sees me.

"Who are you? What are you doing here?" he gasps.

I eye my gun, turning it over in my hand. "I'd love to be the one to really give you what you deserve, but unfortunately, I'm on a time crunch. So this will have to be quick."

"What do you mean?" He staggers toward his nightstand.

I hold up his cell phone, not turning around to face him. "A gun in the bedside table would have been a better option, but either way, looks like you're stuck with me," I say.

"What do you want? I'll give you the combination to the safe and you can leave." I really wish he would just shut up.

"I'm here because of Allie," I shout, standing and facing him as he huddles against the wall.

The shock is evident on his face and he stands taller, stepping away from the wall. "What about Allison?" Oh, no wonder she hates being called Allison.

"What about her?" I yell. "You traded her to Mikhail Belov to save your ass! Did you know that he sent someone to kidnap her in her home?"

"Who are you?" he asks, narrowing his eyes at me.

"I'm her Old Man." I'm vibrating with rage, and I take another step toward him, stepping around the side of the bed.

He scoffs, a look of disgust smearing his face. "Of course, she would get tangled up with biker scum. She's one of your club whores, isn't she? Being passed around between all of you," he sneers.

Everything goes black, and by the time I come back to, Alexei is against the wall with a broken nose and clawing at my hand around his throat. Laughing wildly, I shake my head. "She's not a whore. She's the Queen, and you're dying tonight because you crossed her and you crossed me." Panic shines in his eyes, eyes that are nothing like Allie's, as I squeeze his throat tighter, my fingers digging in at the back of his neck. "How could you do this to your daughter?" I ask. He glares at me, and I know he's going to be stubborn, so I let go of him, letting him sag against the wall as I squeeze his cheeks hard enough to pop open his mouth. I shove the barrel of my gun into his mouth, knocking some of his teeth in the process. I shove it as far as it will go. "Answer me!" I yell as he starts to cough and nod his head.

Pulling out the gun, he sputters and coughs but when he gets it under control he glares at me again. "She was always a disappointment and inconvenience to me. I was glad to finally be rid of her, just like her cheating mother."

That last part catches me by surprise. Allie's never talked about her mom. "What did you do to her mother?" Alexei doesn't say anything, only an evil smile answers me. I already know what that means. He either killed her or had her killed. "You're a piece of shit, and you deserve so much worse than this," I say before yanking him by his throat and tossing him behind me. I turn around as he stumbles forward and aim the gun at the back of his head, squeezing the trigger twice and watching the bullets hit the target. One goes through his throat and the other into his back.

When he falls to the floor, I step over to him and pull some gloves on. Bending over him, I dig through the hole in his back and fish out the bullet, then while he bleeds out, I look around the room for the other one and the casings. I agreed that Mikhail could take care of the body, but I'm not leaving my bullet in him for them to use against me later.

I resume my seat on the bench and watch Alexei take his last gasping breath. Quick and easy.

I STRUGGLE to pick the lock, but finally, I jiggle it unlocked and push the front door open. Standing, I come face to face with the barrel of a gun pressing into my forehead and glaring green eyes staring back at me.

"Knock it off, asshole." I whack the gun away from my face.

Mason sets the gun on the table by the door and crosses his arms. "What are you doing here, Saint?"

I sigh and look down at the floor. I knew this was a terrible idea, but I had to come. Guilt has been eating me up the entire flight back to Washington. Guilt for killing Allie's father, guilt for being so fucking awful to her. When I heard Alexei call her by her full name—the disdain that was in his voice—I tasted ash for every time I called her by it. The thought of being anything like her disgusting, piece of shit father, made me sick to my stomach. "I need to talk to her."

He shakes his head. "Not tonight, Saint. She doesn't need to fight with you tonight."

"No fighting," I plead. "I just want to apologize."

Mason bites his lip, taking a step back, and turns around to walk to Allie's room. I follow behind him, only now noticing that he's shirtless and only has lounge shorts on. I want to strangle him, but I push that feeling down.

He knocks gently on a door. "Al, it was just Saint. He wants to talk if that's okay?"

The door unlocks, and Allie opens it, her face is clear of makeup and she's wearing a silk tank top and short pajama set. Mason walks to the bed and sits down and I face Allie, unsure what to say now that I'm here.

"I'm sorry for what I did tonight," I start.

Allie shrugs one shoulder. "I'm fine. He deserved it."

"It's still shitty." I lick my lips.

Allie crossed her arms over her chest and stares at the floor. "Is that it?"

I swallow the lump in my throat, wishing that I could just throw her over my shoulder and take her to a place where none of this existed, not our bickering, my anger toward her, her father, none of it. "Yeah, I guess so." I turn around and step out of the door.

"Saint," she whispers, but I hear the plea in her voice.

Biting my lip, I shake my head. "You chose him, Allie," I say gently. I'm not angry anymore. I've accepted it, and I just want her to be happy now.

"I didn't choose Mason over you," she says quickly. "I never chose anyone, I wanted you both. I still do."

I turn around and look at Mason, but he just watches me calmly. No anger or jealousy on his face. "What, so you're with both of us? How does that work?" I am a little more irritable than I mean to be.

Allie bites her lip and casts a quick glance at Mason. "I don't know, but we could figure it out, together."

"Allie," I sigh.

"Just because I feel something for Mason, doesn't mean I feel anything less for you. I love you both. Together you make up both sides of my heart. I feel like I can't fully breathe when I'm apart from one of you. Please, Saint. We've tried not being together and that's only hurt us both, why can't we try it?"

Hearing her tell me she loves me is like a bandage wrapping around my heart. I can feel it stitching itself back together at the thought of holding her again, at having her by my side properly. She was my salvation once, and I know that hasn't changed, no matter how angry I've been with her. "What do you want me to do, my Queen?" I let all of the weight that's been weighing on me go, letting my shoulders relax, and my mind releases all of the doubts and sorrow over Ronan.

"Stay with us for tonight, and we can go from there." Allie grabs my arms, gently pulling me into her room.

I look over at Mason as he slides back on the bed, getting under the comforter and holding it open for us. Allie has made it perfectly clear that she's not giving Mason up, and I guess if I have to share her with anybody, I'd rather it be a brother. And Mase isn't the worst choice between them. I don't know what we're getting ourselves into. I don't know how this will work, but if it'll be better than the hell that I've been living without her, then maybe I should try.

I watch Allie's ass as she climbs into the bed, her ass hanging out of the bottom of the shorts as she crawls into the middle of the bed. I catch Mason's eye as she lays down, her back to him. He smiles softly like he's trying to hide it.

I pull my shirt off, toss it aside, and then unbutton my jeans and step out of them with my shoes and socks. "Leave your shorts on, we can't both not have pants on, and I'm not above smothering you in your sleep."

He chuckles. "You'll have to get used to it, I like sleeping naked."

Blinking, I bend down to pick my shirt up. Nope, I'm out. "He's joking!" Allie rushes, shooting up and climbing across the bed to grab my shirt from me.

Mason cackles on the bed and Allie gently pulls the shirt from my hand, dropping it back to the floor and pulling me to the bed.

I keep my hand in hers and our eyes locked as I climb into the bed with them.

We lay down, Allie sliding an extra pillow over for me. "Turn over, I want to hold you," I whisper.

She smiles widely and does exactly as I ask. I wrap my arms around her stomach and slide into her back, pressing myself against her fully. I don't want any space between us. There's already been too much.

I feel Mason's hand slide onto Allie's waist and hear a sniffle.

Mason and I both lean up and look down at Allie.

"What's wrong, Solnyshko?" Mason asks, and I look up at him, confused. What the fuck does that mean?

"Nothing's wrong," Allie lets out a wet laugh. "I'm so happy. I never thought I could have you both." She reaches up to cup our cheeks. "And now you're both here."

"We're not going anywhere, Al. We're right here." Mason looks at me pointedly. "Right, Saint?"

Allie looks over at me, a hopeful gleam in her wet eyes. "I'm not going anywhere, my Queen."

Allie wipes her eyes dry and Mason and I lay down again, resuming our previous position.

I hear Allie sigh happily and burrow further into the bed. I realize that this may not be the worst thing in the world, but we definitely need a bigger bed if we're going to continue to share.

40

MASON

As much as I don't want to, I pull myself out of bed, kissing Allie gently on the lips before I crawl out. Saint's arms are wrapped around her, and surprisingly, it wasn't weird sharing her or the bed with him last night. We got comfortable quickly and fell asleep. I'd much rather lay in bed with them until they both wake up, but maybe it's better Saint wake up without me here; ease him in slowly. Allie barely opens her eyes to whisper goodbye, and I get dressed and head out.

I want to keep tabs on what Mikhail does with Alexei. Saint said he took any evidence that could lead back to him, but I want to be sure that Mikhail doesn't try to hang us out to dry.

The clubhouse is quiet this early in the morning, so I head upstairs and push open my door. I know Allie is more comfortable in her home, and there's just something about being in your own space. This is mine. Maybe soon we can all figure out a place where we're all comfortable. A home.

I sit down at my computer and get everything turned on, bending down to grab an energy drink from the mini fridge under my desk.

I barely get my computer online when an alert comes across

my screen for movement at the front gate. Thinking it's just one of the guys, I briefly glance over at the monitor with the camera feed on it.

My heart sinks when I see a girl with light pink hair huddled on the ground in front of the gate in the fetal position. A pickup is speeding away and there's a dark spot on the side of her head that looks like blood in the camera, but I can't be certain from here. I dart out of the room, banging on Jack and Nox's doors as I sprint down the stairs and to the gate. The guys aren't too far behind me, both shirtless and in shorts, my banging on their doors having woken them up.

We get the gate open and check the girl over. It's Peyton, one of the bartenders from the Second Circle, the strip club that the club owns. She's unconscious, and if it weren't for her colored hair, I probably wouldn't have recognized her broken and beaten face. She has bruises, cuts, and scrapes across every visible inch of her body, which is just about everywhere.

"Oh shit," Jack gasps.

Nox runs back to get his truck so we can take her to the hospital when my phone starts to vibrate in my hand. Allie's calling.

Call me paranoid, but a beaten girl showing up on our doorstep and then my sleeping girlfriend calling me kind of sets off panic bells in my head. "What's going on, Solnyshko?" I answer quickly.

"Where are you?" Allie rushes, panic thick in her voice.

I stand and look around the compound and down the street. "The clubhouse, what's going on, Allie?"

"You need to get out of there! Now!" Allie yells.

"What's going on, Allie?" I say, a little more forceful this time.

"Saint got a video of you killing Ronan. He's coming for you, Mase."

To be continued...

ACKNOWLEDGMENTS

I'm so sorry for everyone that loved Ronan. I will admit that through OTS and WS, I did try to make him a very lovable character. I wanted his death to hurt a little. I never anticipated him to earn such a big place in some reader's hearts.

I also didn't anticipate to go into This Mess with so much anger and pain. I knew that Saint was going to struggle with Ronan's death—-I wrote the first chapter while I was writing OTS—but as the story developed, I realized that I was harboring a lot of emotions over my mother's death. I'm sorry if Saint's and my emotions brought up something uncomfortable for you. Writing This Mess ending up being really healing for me, and although I don't think I will ever completely heal from losing my mom the way I did, it did help a lot.

As always, thank you so much to Emi for taking my unedited thoughts and turning them into a legible story. I value your opinions so much, and I trust you with one of the most important things to me. I love you, and I could never trust someone as much as you with my characters!

Kortnee, thank you for being my friend even when I suck at texting back! I love you forever and I can't wait for us to catch a Seahawks game together!

Kiersten. I never knew that I could feel so close to someone who lives so far away! Thank you for always encouraging me, cheering me on, distracting me when my mind isn't nice to me, and being my sounding board for covers and story choices. Your song recs kick ass and save me when I'm trying to search through my liked playlist on Spotify. You always know exactly what I'm looking for and save my ass! Love ya! Orcas 4 lyfe <3

Bethany

ABOUT THE AUTHOR

To discuss spoilers, theories, cliffhanger rants, and read deleted scenes for Will Survive, join our Facebook group, The DO Chapel.

You can also follow me on TikTok @queenb17, Instagram @bethanydawnauthor, and my Facebook page @BethanyDawnAuthor